Punkin Strudel Mayhem

Map of Leavensport, Ohio

Leavensport, Ohio

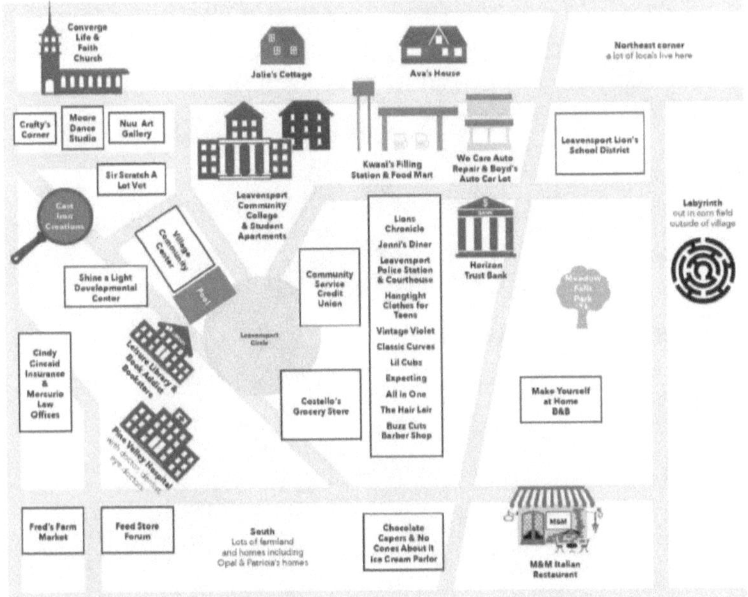

Punkin Strudel Mayhem

A Holiday Novella 7.5 in The Cast Iron Skillet Mystery Series

Jodi Rath

rights is appreciated.

https://www.jodirath.com

Note from the Publisher: The recipes contained in this book are to be followed precisely as written. Be aware that oven temperatures vary. The publisher and author are not responsible for your specific health or allergy needs that may require medical supervision. The publisher and author are not responsible for any adverse reactions to the recipes contained in this book or series.

Cover Design by Karen Phillips at Phillips Coverswww.PhillipsCovers.com

Edited by Rebecca Grubb at Sterling Words www.sterlingwords.com

Formatted by Merry Bond at Anessa bookshttp://anessabooks.com

When black cats roam and pumpkins gleam, may luck be yours on Halloween.

Dedication

This book was so much fun to write. Halloween has been my favorite holiday for as long as I can remember. I look forward to decorating for it every year—I start early and leave the decorations up a tad too long.

This book is dedicated to all the readers out there who have been beyond supportive of my writing this series. I'm not sure I can fully convey what it means to me. Writing is a lonely business, but I'm that girl. I've always retreated to my room or office to read, write, journal, research, or mess around with sketching and art projects. My point is, I never thought I'd be able to make it as a full-time writer. Granted, my business is more than writing—I still have a hand in education because I won't ever be able to fully let go of the teacher in me—but being able to diversify my writing—it's a life-long dream come true. YOU all, the readers, are the ones who make that possible for me to do. Without your support, I wouldn't be here.

I had NO clue that I'd make so many reader friends through newsletters and social media! Also, I didn't realize how much fun doing newsletters, raffles, and social media posts would be and how well I'd get to know my readers! It's truly become a community in itself and I can't imagine ever living without all of you now! Why do I keep using exclamation marks?!? My editor is not going to be happy! LOL! [Editor's note: please make it stop]

My point is, I wanted to do something fun and special for all of you SUPER faithful readers of the entire series out there. So here is a little hint: as you read this book, you will notice that some of the words are in the CHILLER font. Some of that is onomatopoeia, where characters are making noises, but any words that are in the CHILLER font and are NOT noises are clues to the mystery themes running through the entire series. If you feel like a super sleuth, make a note of these words/phrases. As the series continues to its end, you will be able to take some guesses as to how things will unfold and I'll do raffles for the super sleuths to win prizes.

Also, keep your eyes peeled for the BIGGEST raffle YET coming for the last book in the series. Those of you who follow me in the newsletter or on social media know we've done a ton of amazing raffles to date—so you can imagine that the last one will be a doozy if you care to play!

If you're someone new to the series, no worries—there is plenty of time for you to catch up so you can get in on the mystery-sleuthing action! Links to our newsletter and our social media community are at the end of this book.

My eternal gratitude to every single reader out there!

The Leavensport Crew

Two Protagonists:

Jolie Tucker-Meiser—Co-owner of Cast Iron Creations, born in the village, best friend of Ava, granddaughter of Opal, daughter of Patty.

Ava Martinez—Co-owner of Cast Iron Creations, born in the village, best friend of Jolie, girlfriend of Delilah, sister of Lolly, daughter of Sophia and Thiago.

Jolie Tucker's Family:

Grandma Opal—Jolie's grandma, housewife who helped Jolie and Ava start Cast Iron Creations with her cast-iron skillet recipes.

Aunt Fern—Jolie's wacky, unpredictable aunt, sister to Patty, man-hungry.

Patty—Jolie's mom.

Mike—Jolie's stepdad who was like her real father. He passed away when she was in high school.

Chuck—Jolie's biological father.

Eddie—uncle to Jolie. He, wife Shelly, and their five kids were estranged from the family for decades.

Wylie—uncle to Jolie.

Detective Mick Meiser (formerly Milano)—

Jolie's husband, from Tri-City, transferred career to Leavensport. Changed his name to separate himself from the Milano family.

Ava Martinez's Family:

Thiago Martinez—Ava's dad; her family lived in Leavensport her entire life but are from Santo Domingo. Theo, his son-in-law, had to relocate to the Dominican Republic for work several years ago.

Sophia Martinez—Ava's mom.

Lolly Sanchez—Ava's sister.

Theo Sanchez—Lolly's husband.

Delilah Sampson-Martinez—Sister of Bradley, village artist, wife of Ava.

Detective Mick Meiser:

Maria Milano—Mick's sister.

Maddox Milano—Mick's dad.

Maya Milano—Mick's mom.

Imelda—Italian princess who is a love interest from Mick's past.

Leavensport Villagers:

Bradley—Brother of Delilah, village journalist

Bea and Earl Seevers—staple couple in the village who adore Jolie and Ava.

Chief Teddy Tobias—Police chief of Leavensport and born in the village, best friend of

Keith

Keith—Ex-boyfriend of Jolie, born in the village, best friend of Teddy—now a police officer in Leavensport

Lydia—Jolie's frenemy, village nurse, best friend of Betsy, born in the village, Monty's mother

Betsy—Owns Chocolate Capers, best friend of Lydia, born in the village. Her aunt was Ellie Siler who was Grandma Opal's best friend.

Bobby Zane—new principal of the Leavensport Lions High School—silent partner in Carlos' upcoming new restaurant, Carlos' Hot Tamales

Nina Sanchez—Mother of Luis and owns a new bakery in town

Ryder Chen—new chef taking over for Carlos at Cast Iron Creations—currently in training

Tri-City Natives

Jackson Nestle—Unscrupulous political associate of Mayor Cardinal from Tri-City, owner of Nestle Construction

Caleb and Asher—work for Nestle Construction

Pria—a past teen counselor/advocate in Tri-City.

Chapter One

October in Leavensport was similar to Salem, Massachusetts in that our villagers LOVED to decorate and pay tribute to the witches, goblins, and spirits of the dead—a tad too much at times. Don't get me wrong, I adore a witch costume as much as the next gal, but Grandma Opal, my mom, and Aunt Fern have dressed up as the witches from *Macbeth* to recite the famous "Double, double, toil and trouble," incantation every single year since I can remember. They are always trying to get me to join in the family fun and it drives me up the wall. I continually tell them there are only three witches and so far, that's saved me. Halloween has been my favorite holiday since I was a child and that makes the village's annual All Hallows' Eve bash less annoying. It helps that wearing a costume gives me that feeling of anonymity that is basically the definition of my "comfort zone"—not to mention chocolate and I have a passionate relationship.

This year was no different. I started out excited about Halloween, then things took a turn for the worse. The twin monsters I'm carrying around in my stomach were ready to pop out, and, in my opinion, my due date of November fifth couldn't come soon enough. Ava and Delilah were only carrying one each inside them and they were both getting crabbier by the minute. The Ohio sky matched my mood—misty, gray, and rumbling, threatening to cry all over the villagers of Leavensport. My own mood swings had been out of control for the last week and my vivid dreams had turned into intense nightmares. My OB Dr. Snyder assured me this was normal for a woman carrying twins. Actually, I believe he sang out, "especially those due around the witches' feast of the dead."

Dr. S liked to find the melody in life and typically sang good news or things he found funny. I didn't always see the humor in that—but I was grumpier than normal with the twins having a kickboxing match in my stomach.

Today, I could tell it was going to be *one of those days.* I woke to water dripping on my face. Our new roof had sprung a leak right over the spot where I laid my head to rest. After placing a large bucket where my pillow should be, I texted Mick to let him know, and being the best husband in the world, he promised to meet the roofers that afternoon. I forced myself to not start the day in a bad mood and began humming "Monster Mash" as I went to the bathroom to brush my teeth. Dr. Snyder would be so proud.

Bobbi Jo, our bobtail kitty, jumped up on the counter and butted her cute little calico head into my hand, launching my toothbrush into the toilet. I may have used a few…unladylike…words, but I chalked it up as—well, like I said, *one of those days.* Rather than go to work with bad breath and gritty teeth, I opted to use my finger to at least freshen my mouth up a bit and used three times my usual amount of mouthwash.

Next, the hot water cut out halfway through my shower while the shampoo was bubbled up on my curly mop. I squealed as the freezing water gushed over my head and body and the twins resumed their kicking in protest.

The rest of the morning—at least getting ready to leave the house—went smoothly. I put on my favorite maternity dress—black with orange pumpkin novelty prints and cobwebbed pattern over it—and headed out. As I drove to the restaurant I co-owned with Ava, Cast Iron Creations, I turned on some relaxing, meditative music I'd found to help calm my anxiety for the last several months. I did as my YouTube videos instructed and took deep breaths, visualizing embracing the good with each inhale and releasing the bad with each exhale. My family didn't realize that both Ava and I knew about the "surprise" baby shower they were holding after our shift today. I knew they wanted to get the baby shower in a few days before Leavensport's annual All Hallows' Eve bash took place.

I felt my body begin to unclench more and the twins settled down as I neared the center of the village. People were out in the sprinkling rain, putting up decorative cobwebs with large spiders in the center, witches' hats, cauldrons, and golden goblets with green gunk that appeared to be bubbling over all along the streets—OH CRAP! I was supposed to tell Grandma Opal to dig out our cast-iron cauldrons from her basement to use around the restaurant.

I clicked the button to make a phone call in the Honda CR-V. "Call Grandma," I said.

"Calling Ava," my robotic car spirit spoke back.

"What?" I cut it off. "CALL GRAND-MA!" I screamed at her, then took a breath.

"Calling—" she started before I screeched the brakes and felt the seat belt cut into my chest, "—Ava."

"What on Earth?" I checked behind me, then put my flashers on and got out of the car.

Three black kittens sat in the middle of the road, staring up at me, mewing. They looked exactly like Ava's three babies, Luna, Lily, and Lulu. Mick and I had eight cats of our own at home. We were both...well...*kitty whipped*, to say the least.

"Hi, babies—are you Lily, Luna, and Lulu?" I asked, attempting to bend down to them but forgetting my knees didn't function that way now that I'm pregnant.

The tiniest of the crew with a small white mark

on her neck just like Ava's little Lily came right up to me as I bent down to pick her up. She purred loudly, leaning into my chest.

"Ooooooh," I cooed.

Someone honked behind me and I turned and glared at them and then quickly turned back to make sure the other two didn't take off. They had crept up to my feet, nearly climbing my maternity dress.

"Move it!" yelled Asher from his Nestle Construction truck. He worked for Jackson Nestle—a man I despised.

"Go around me, jerk face!" I yelled at him, then picked up the other two kitties with my free hand and with great effort, curled my one spare pinkie finger under the handle to open the back door of the CR-V. I carefully balanced the writhing armloads of cats as I opened the door with my hip and stomach (thanks for the assist, twins!) and finally stashed the three kitties in one of the many empty cardboard boxes there—there was ample evidence in my back seat that I had a bit of an...Amazon addiction.

I flopped back in the driver's seat with a groan and put the car in gear, pulling over to the side of the road.

"Hello—Jolie—JOLIE!" Ava bellowed from the car speaker.

"Are your three girls at home?" I asked.

"Of course they are! Where else would they

be?" Ava grumped at me.

"I'm staring at them right now, Jolie," I heard Delilah mutter.

"Why?" Ava barked.

Boy, not a good day for those two either.

"Nothing. I'm going to be late," I said. "I have to run to Dr. Libby's office first. I gotta go. I'll tell you about it later." I glanced behind me to make sure no one was coming before I pulled back onto the road.

Suddenly, one of the kittens jumped out of the box onto my shoulder, digging her claws into me. I shrieked and jerked the wheel as a large silver blur came out of nowhere and slammed into the side of my car, then everything went black.

Chapter Two

The annual All Hallows' Eve bash was in full swing.
The first thing I rushed for was the candied apples.
Betsy had quadruple-chocolate-caramel apples with
peanuts and little dots of heavenly chocolate stuck
over the entire apple. It was like the sweet, red fruit
was guarded by layers and layers of gooey caramel
and rich, decadent chocolate and I didn't care if I
ever got to the fruit.

Three small ghosts floated past me, giggling
uncontrollably.

"Hey, how are you kids doing that?" I called
out, wondering if they had hidden hoverboards
under their sheets—which, brilliant!

I took another large bite, still getting nothing
but caramel and chocolate, and closed my eyes and
moaned, rubbing my belly. When I opened my baby
blues, more than a dozen mummies were waving at
me and free-falling from the sky. *Huh, that's weird.*
Their tattered, dirty rags hung loose in the breeze

against the skies that had suddenly grayed over. A light mist came down and my first thought was to protect my candied apple, but I noticed the mist falling from the sky was like a light blue cotton-candied haze.

I jerked my head around, searching for some techno-gadgety machine that Aunt Fern or Mayor Nalini had purchased to make the wonderful sprinkling rain of sugary sweetness fall from the sky, but I couldn't locate it. *Who cares? It's so cool!*

A sign caught my eye and grabbed my attention as if I was in a trance.

Madame Esme Emerald's Psychic Readings. What does your future hold?

I walked out of the light blue mist and through the entrance of a large purple and sea-witch green tent. The interior was dark except for the flickering light from candles sitting on gargoyle statues. Long, flowing, rich-colored fabrics were draped over tables.

"Come in, Jolie. I've been waiting for you," a deep, husky voice called from behind a curtain.

I took two steps forward, pushing the velvety royal purple curtain to the side, first noticing mirrors everywhere I turned. Next, I saw a seated figure in the dimness and stepped closer.

"Please set your treat on the golden plate here at the table." A weathered beauty with long, blue-streaked hair extended a hand covered with tattoos toward the empty seat that awaited me.

I gazed longingly at my crunchy chocolatey treat, then slowly set it on the white napkin on the rustic golden platter. I took my time laboriously lowering myself into the seat.

"I am Madame Esme Emerald. I see you are due soon." She eyed my stomach.

"I don't have to pay you for that, do I?" My smart-alecky attitude seemed to intensify the longer the pregnancy lasted.

Madame Esme made a huffing sound that turned into a low, deep screech. Then she lifted a russet arm that jangled with gemstone-adorned hippie bracelets. "You, my dear, do not need to make payments to the spirits that wish to speak to you. Not at this juncture, at least. Your future will determine that fate."

I bit my lower lip and glanced to the right, where two candles began flickering wildly. Suddenly, they both snuffed out, leaving a spicy-scented, mystic-blue ring of smoke floating to the top of the tent, where it dissipated. "There are spirits who want to speak to me?"

Before I thought about it, I began to reach for the chocolate apple but stopped mid-reach when Madame Esme's eyes rolled back into her head, her eyelids fluttering like butterflies. Suddenly, I heard voices ringing out from all directions. I stiffened and looked around.

The sound gave me the strangest sensation—the voices I heard were familiar, but since they were all talking at once, I couldn't distinguish one from the other. I began to see throngs of blurry people, moving together in one direction, toward a tunnel with a light at the end of it. Their colored costumes created rainbow prisms swirling around my eyes. I felt a wave of nausea—my head was swimming, my stomach churning. Then, a sudden shock coursed through me and sent my body slamming up against a hard surface, but somehow bouncing my head against a puffy cloud.

BEEEP.

I turned my head to see where the noise was coming from, but I couldn't see.

"JOLEEEEEE!" Ava screamed as if someone was murdering her.

"Ava?" I panicked. What was happening to me? Why couldn't I see her?

"Baby, it's me." Mick's voice was steady, firm, and demanding. "Come back to me. I refuse to let you go. I can't live without you." I felt his hand in mine, then heard someone talking to him.

"Get them out of here. NOW!" a voice that sounded like Dr. Snyder yelled—the chipper melodic songs I was used to hearing was replaced by a commanding voice barking orders.

Suddenly, I was hovering over my body, which

was lying in a bed with Dr. Snyder, several nurses, and men and women in scrubs hooking me up to machines. I was unconscious and had a massive head wound. There were some glass fragments and blood—I looked down at my stomach, willing the twins to be okay.

A man in scrubs was gripping my husband's arms, pushing him out the door while a woman in a mask and gloves spoke softly to Ava—trying unsuccessfully to calm her down. Her eyes were bulging out of her head and her arms reached for my body as she screamed, "NOOOOOOooooooooooooo…" Her voice trailed off as several orderlies worked to remove her from the room.

I tried to reach for them from where I floated above, but my arm was airy and light.

Chapter Three

My eyes had been tightly shut and my entire body was rigid as a concrete statue standing upright. I remembered my YouTube meditations and sucked in a large, icy breath of air and released it slowly, opening my eyes to see my breath make a puffy white fog in a darkened enclosure.

Something wasn't right. I couldn't shake the sensation as I took a few uncertain steps on the dirt floor. A breeze kicked up some dust, making me wheeze a bit. Down a long tunnelway, I saw a glow that was growing brighter by the second. Something was rushing toward me. I covered my eyes from the glare and felt my dress blow back against my legs. I looked down to find myself hovering over the ground in a white gown. I gasped. *What the heck?* Besides the hovering, my body appeared to be normal, but something was definitely wrong, I just couldn't put my finger on it. Just then, I glanced up to see a big, sleek, futuristic hovercar whoosh through me as if I was made of air. I gasped and without thinking, clutched at my middle, cupping my hands protectively around my lower abdomen. *That's weird, that hovercar should have obliterated my entire body. Why did I bother to grab my stomach?* I stared hard at it. What was I trying to protect? *Am I dreaming or dead? Why am I so disoriented?*

But just as I was beginning to remember a few blurry details, I became aware of the clamor of voices and the distant glow of colored lights from a long distance down the tunnel. Then, somehow, just by thinking about it, I was there. There, in the tunnel, underground, was a casino! Neon pink, glowing yellow, vivid green, and bright orange lasers sliced through the darkness, bouncing beams off of the tunnel walls. Distance and time seemed to be playing tricks on my mind.

The elevated foundation of the casino sat inside an enormous ornate siena marble fountain so that the pool of water surrounded the outside of the casino like the moat of some otherworldly fortress. The rim of the marble pool was studded with spouts that sent arcs of water into the air, refracting the lasers and creating a cascade of multicolored, glittering drops. I didn't see the entrance—it appeared that the whole casino was surrounded by a sparkling wall of water.

Somehow, though, I could see through the casino walls with my mind, and inside, swarms of people sat at poker tables and slot machines that looked like they were from a sci-fi movie, scanning in their fingerprints to continue spinning the wheel of loss. *Underground. Illegal gambling.* The thought popped into my brain like a message. I became anxious momentarily thinking, *what is happening to me? Am I dead?*

Before complete panic set in, I became fascinated at how people were entering the casino. High-tech rainbow-prismed hoverboards glided above the water at the outer edge of the fountain as small spouts of water around the fountain sprayed out rainbow mist that lifted visitors from the ground to the entrance of the casino. I watched as a woman in a snake costume used a small hand remote to bring a hoverboard to her. A clear dome protected her from the water as she stepped onto the board. She used the device in her hand to steer the board through the jets of water to the entrance, where the dome opened and she exited the hoverboard and walked inside.

Since I was able to float in this new realm, I glided around the fountain, noticing three bronze sculptures of women positioned evenly around the casino. One woman had long dreadlocks spread up in the air as if a strong wind had lifted them and the water spouted from the tip of each dread, spraying every which way. Sculpted flames soared over the first statue's hand, spraying out a red mist that took on a smokey look. I drifted slowly around the fountain. The second bronze woman was an angel. Her large wings lifted and fell as water sprayed from the wingtips, suggesting a movement of celestial bodies of water. The third woman stood, naked, holding over her head a chunk of ice. Mist lifted from its surface, giving the illusion of frozen vapor.

I looked through the walls of the casino to see two women who seemed like they were plotting something. *Wait, I know them.* I mentally forced myself to enter the casino, floating straight through the walls, toward the two women who seemed vaguely familiar. Goosebumps formed on my arms and spread across my body as I realized the powers I held. Inside the casino, the air vibrated with sinister energy. My body cinched up and I felt a wave of nausea. My muscles twitched and cramped. I rubbed my arms and glanced around for the women. *There they were.* One woman had buzzed-off hair and the other had short, black, wavy hair. The latter woman turned, and her vivid, sharp eyes seemed to stare straight through me.

"I've never been happier to see anyone in my life," the woman with piercing eyes said to me.

"You—you can see me?" I asked. Then noticed they were drifting off the ground too.

"Be careful, girl," came Madame Esme Emerald's voice, seeming to come from within my soul. "Do not associate with the dead too much. Your fate has yet to be determined."

I watched the two apparitions in front of me to see if they had heard her low, earthy, trembling voice. They hadn't reacted. *The dead? My fate has not been determined yet.* I began trying to put the pieces together when my thoughts were interrupted by the voice of the woman with short black hair.

"Shall we play a game, Bonnie?" The woman with the piercing eyes grinned roguishly, then floated over a heavyset red-headed couple sitting at the slot machines.

I could overhear the couple's conversation.

"Ed, please stop. We can sell the place and at this point break even. I've got our twins on the way. I'm begging you not to do this!"

"Oh, let's play," Bonnie said as the other spirit reached for Ed's hand to make him pull the lever.

Don't do it, ED! I pressed my index fingers into my forehead, willing Ed to make the right decision.

"I told you once, child. No more warnings!" Madame Esme's voice blasted through me and I flew through the casino walls and out into the tunnel and my body bounced hard against a rock.

I opened my eyes and gasped. Reality had shifted without warning. Suddenly, I was somewhere else, but it was a place that was familiar. I was above ground now, in the middle of Leavensport, standing on the street as the villagers decorated for Halloween. I glanced down at my hands on my abdomen. My stomach was round— four times the size it had been in the tunnels. I raised my head slowly as long, loose, dark-blonde curls bounced around my cheeks. A red Honda CR-V was coming down the street.

I shook my head slowly as if I knew what was

coming, wishing the vehicle would turn around. "Go home!" I willed.

The car screeched to a halt, and I looked for three black kittens in the road, but instead, my Grandma Opal stepped out and stood in her favorite apron reading NO B*TCHIN IN GRANDMA'S KITCHEN!

Suddenly I was in her kitchen. "What are you making?" I asked, hurrying toward the stove and smelling her pineapple upside-down cake right away.

She didn't seem to be able to hear me.

"Grandma. Grand-ma!" I tried again. Nothing.

A large silver construction truck barreled straight for her.

"GRANDMA!" I screamed, running toward her.

"I WARNED YOU!" Madame Esme's voice surged within me, and I was jerked back to the seat in her tent.

I licked my dry lips and glanced around the tent of mirrors, panic-stricken, but not sure why. I tried to remember the events of the past few minutes, but it felt like trying to remember a dream after waking up. It quickly unraveled into nothing.

"Madame Esme, may I have some water please?" I asked.

"Of course, child." She turned to a large clay pot full of water that sat on a small table that appeared out of nowhere next to her. She poured some water into an ancient-looking, rusty goblet that had sparkly gems shining through the rust. "Ah, you see through the rust. Very interesting indeed," she said, reaching across the table to hand me the drink.

The water was icy cold, and I drank it down in what felt like one large gulp. It was the best-tasting water I'd ever had. "I see something sparkly," I shrugged my shoulders then wiped my mouth, handing back the cup.

"You keep that, child. It could come in handy later on during your journey."

I put the goblet in my lap. "Why am I here?"

"How should I know? To get a reading is all I can think of." Madame Esme grinned and reached for my hand, placing it on a crystal ball that appeared out of thin air. "Child, leave both hands on the crystal ball while I pull your card." She split the deck once, then once more, and then pulled a card and held it momentarily to her heart before turning it over. I stared down at the card—on it, two dolphins created a circle. "The moon in reverse," she whispered. I met her eyes. They were stormy. "Fear, deception, anxiety, misunderstanding, and misinterpretation."

Under my hands, purple and pink swirled like a nebula inside the crystal ball. Madame Esme Emerald began to change. Her long, dark locks of hair slowly shifted to cornflower, baby, and azure blue. Tiny, bright-yellow stars shimmered throughout her waist-length hair. Her high cheekbones and narrow chin receded in front of me as if I were watching aging in reverse—rosy pink bloomed on her tawny-beige Cherokee cheeks and large gold hoops strung with turquoise circles and wooden arrows dangled from her earlobes to her shoulder.

"Great, Great, Great!" I squealed, feeling my pigtails bounce up and down as my chubby toddler hands reached for her. I suddenly became conscious of knowledge without needing to learn it. I knew who she was. My great-great-great-granny Esme reached for me from across the table, smiling broadly and picking me up in her strong arms.

"Jolie, who knew we'd ever meet like this, my child? You will grow to be strong like your people. But make no mistake, you will be tested in your life—men will bring harm and pain, family will take on shadows, battles and wars will be fought. Never forget family is more than the blood that runs through your veins."

"Mike!" I babbled.

Great-Granny Esme smiled and nodded down at me. "He is only one example, my dear. You will have no siblings by blood, but Ava, Delilah, Bradley, Keith, and Mick will all become connections that are as strong as family bonds. You are blessed, child. Don't allow the world's pain to pull you underground. Stay above and feel the rain on your face."

I raised my chin as a cool, misty rain began, allowing it to wash over me and feeling the warmth and love of my Great-Granny Esme's spirit infuse me.

When I opened my eyes, I was drifting over myself in a hospital room again. I could hear Dr. Delagada talking next to me. "Mick, you need to go home. The stress of being here and seeing her and your twins like this is too much for your MS. I'm afraid you are going to have a setback."

"I am NOT leaving her or them."

Okay, I'm somewhere in the middle— unconscious in the world I know, as my spirit wanders around another realm? This was my best guess. I needed to utilize my newfound powers to help my husband.

Baby, go home. We need you strong for us, I tried to say to my husband. He wasn't hearing me. Stubborn man! *Oh well, no worries.* I sent my thoughts toward his doctor.

"Mick, think about what Jolie would say to you right now," Dr. Delagada started.

I smiled to myself. *Woman's intuition.*

"What?" My crank of a husband grumbled at the woman I was using to send him a message.

I clapped my phantom hands at his face to get his attention.

Mick's head jerked up and he waited for Dr. Delagada to speak.

"You know as well as I do that she'd tell you that she and those girls of yours need you to be at your strongest for them when they are better. Now, listen to your wife, go home, take a hot shower, feed your cats, get something to eat with some chocolate for dessert, then get some sleep. I'll be here in the morning watching over the kids."

"Jolie?" Mick stared at Dr. Delagada.

"What?" Dr. Delagada seemed confused.

My eyes darted from left to right in shock at my powers.

"Wicked girl, leave the humans be!" The older version of Great-Granny Esme's spirit was next to mine as she clapped and stomped a native dance and then held my hands to stop me from doing more.

"I'm sorry. You—you're right. I'm exhausted and she's strong. That's what drew me to her—her strength." Mick took a deep breath and released it, his head drooping and his shoulders sagging as he looked at his hands. "You know, someone who's been through so much could just give up or give in—but she refuses. That strength is a magnet of sorts."

"I'm making a note for the nurse to call and check on you in the morning." She put a hand on his shoulder as he sat holding my hand, staring longingly at me. He gently laid my hand on the bed, and reached his head down to kiss my lips. Then he shifted his head to my stomach and rested it there, singing the twins a funny cat song we had made up for our fur babies. I giggled as tears sprung to my eyes and glanced up at Great-Granny above me in the atmosphere, then back down to Mick.

"Child, a big test is coming up for you. If you want to make it back to him, then don't fail this one."

Chapter Four

I found myself betwixt and in between a lucid dream and what seemed like the real world to me—although as time went on, it became harder and harder for me to know which was which.

I waited and listened for Great-Granny Esme's advice as I watched Mick. He slowly walked out of my hospital room. I tried to float down but felt like someone or something had grabbed my collar and pulled me back out, away into the galaxy.

Time was behaving strangely, twisting and buckling. I was somehow both slowly and quickly flying through space. I snapped out of what felt like an illusion to find myself on a Meadow Falls Park bench, sitting next to a life-sized set of Russian dolls. Much like the walls in the casino, I could see through the doll and see all of them stacked inside one another, creating concentric layers of dolls all the way to a tiny one in the center. They were large, quilted ornament dolls with azure-blue winter dresses studded with small, happy, yellow sunflower decorations. They all wore traditional kokoshnik headdresses.

Next to them sat a gray-haired person dressed in a vampire costume. I couldn't tell the gender of the person in the regalia, but they sat with their arm around the dolls, grinning scornfully at me.

"Who are you?" I demanded.

The boorishly large, creepy grin continued as the figure shrugged and walked off. I continued staring at the dolls able to see through all the layers simultaneously when the top layer came to life, and shape-shifted into a familiar face.

"PRIA!" I yelled and reached out to hug her.

We both reached for each other but got armfuls of space. I stood back and smiled. I still saw her with the short, spiky black hair—there was an angelic glow with bright rainbow prisms shining around her. I couldn't believe how long it had been since I'd seen her last. Pria's murder was the second case Ava and I had taken on a few years back, and one of the most heart-breaking. She was only twenty-six when she was killed, and she had so much to offer as the Tri-City teen counselor-slash-political teen advocate. She was passionate about stopping gentrification in the city to help save homeless teens.

"You don't have your wings or the mark of the vampire on your neck. You must be in the Betwixt and In-Between world right now," Pria grinned excitedly. "I've never met up with one of you before."

"It took me a while to realize that—still—I wasn't completely sure," I said, looking nervously at my fingernails and peeling at the nonexistent coral orange nail polish I still saw there.

"Nah, from what I've heard, it's an extremely confusing place to be—depending on what's happening to your physical body on Earth, that strongly affects your level of confu—"

I snapped my head back as my eyes bulged and grew in size creating an irritating pressure to my skull behind my eyes. "ARRAHHAA!" I hollered. *What's happening to me?*

"Okay, Jolie," Pria said urgently. I felt like she was getting farther away as she spoke. "I know you're scared, but all of this is because you are still connected to the physical world. You're trying to wake up. There's a good chance you'll go back. If you remember what happened to you here, please tell Stef that I'm fine and I hang out in the yard with the groundhog family, deer family, raccoon family, squirrels, chipmunks, and all the birds." Pria's eyes filled until one lone tear overflowed, running down her cheek.

My head shook back and forth, and I came back to Pria momentarily. "I will do my best to remember, I promise." I began to reach for her hand then caught myself and we looked at each other and laughed before my head jerked back again.

I swore I heard Ava chattering on and on about

something. I homed in to try and hear better.

"Delilah says I'm nesting for both of us," said Ava. "I know you, though. You freak out if things aren't organized or if you haven't researched every detail and made every accommodation necessary. So, once I've taken care of everything I do for our little cottage, I go over and do the same at your house. Mick finally went home and got some rest. We've all been worried about him and his health—and of course you and the twins—but I keep telling everyone you all will be fine. But girl—" Ava squeezed my hand. "It's been over twenty-four hours and those kiddos are due soon."

I felt my spirit hovering over my physical form again as my body lay motionless in the hospital bed. I willed my apparition to float under where Ava sat and studied her face upside down. "You look silly like that," I said out loud, even though I knew she couldn't hear me, as I reminisced about how when we were kids we'd make homemade tents out of kitchen chairs, blankets, and umbrella handles.

"Yeah," Ava agreed out of nowhere. "Your face always looked like an upside-down Muppet with your pointy chin and all those moppy blonde curls bouncing up and down."

I grinned, knowing she shared my thought and realizing Great-Granny was right—blood isn't always thicker than water.

"Anyway, I've made sure to do spring cleaning in the fall, making sure our walls, sinks, and surfaces are clean, neat, and baby-proofed. This way, you won't have to worry about it when you get home with the girls. Let's see, I've also been putting safety covers on all our outlets, and ..."

Ava continued chattering about her list of ways she was nesting for both of us when I could have sworn I saw one of the flying mummies smash into the window of my hospital room. I hurried toward the frame and looked out the window, placing my hands on the panes to get a better view. I pressed my hands against the pane, wishing the glass was gone. It vibrated, then took on a strange liquid quality. I stumbled forward for a moment due to my hands passing through the glass as if it wasn't there. *These powers are weird!* The mummy hovered outside the window, face to face with me. The wrappings around its face had come loose and I could see one eye.

I gasped in shock. "Nina Sanchez?" I reached for her hand to help her inside.

"Real funny reaching for my hand," Nina said, hanging onto the windowsill with one mummified hand while using the other to reach into her mummied pocket and pull out a baked good that looked like something from her own bakery to munch.

If Nina had died and was mummified, then I must be way in the future?

I wanted some answers, so I put my fingers to my forehead once again, and concentrated on willing Ava to hear me. She began speaking to my form in the bed. When I opened my eyes to listen to her, I noticed Nina doing a walking dead-style mummy walk down the hallway.

"It was a Nestle Construction truck that hit your CR-V, then swerved and hit Nina Sanchez as she was walking on the sidewalk. She died on impact. Luis is devasted. He's all alone. My family is moving back to the village within the next week and Lolly wants me to get DNA from Luis to see if Theo is his dad. Theo isn't saying much when Lolly questions him about Nina, but it's interesting that her last name is Sanchez. She's wondering if Theo was married before. With all of the crap he's pulled in the past, it wouldn't shock anyone if he had a secret ex-wife.

"On top of that, the Milanos have had a temporary prefab put on their property in the woods by the shelter and they're moving here within the week. Things are chaotic, to say the least, and I've found myself trying to take care of all the things you do at the restaurant and with the PI business. It's a lot. More than I ever knew. Your accident has set a lot in motion in a short amount of time."

She started to choke up and I felt her hand squeeze mine momentarily. "I need you to pull through. I need you and those babies to all be okay. I—just—need you to fight, Jolie. Do you hear me? FIGHT!"

Chapter Five

A distant beep continued to keep rhythm—there was a large, translucent metronome in the sky. I shook my head and slapped my own face to try to wake up. After a moment of this, I scanned the empty sky, but I continued to hear the slightly muffled beep. *Still not awake.* I tried to maneuver myself through space and time by wiggling like a snake, but it suddenly felt impossible. Now the world around me was thick and glue-like as my spirit attempted to move. I hovered helplessly in the air—trying to swim through the fabric of space-time was like drowning in molasses.

I stopped trying to fight through the thick, sticky layers and then found myself high in a tree, resting on a thick cushion of what resembled Alien Tape stuck tight in a branch. Below, I could see people in Leavensport strolling around. Many were in costumes and the streets were decorated with bright orange pumpkins, black spiders, witches' hats, and cast-iron cauldrons were lining the streets and green slime was thrown on windows. I worked to smile through the impenetrable haze that surrounded me.

Two figures hovered near me, unaffected by the heavy glutinous smog. They looked like twins—two Marissas, the owner of the new deep-dish pizza place in town. I tried to furrow my brow but felt like I had just been injected with Botox. I felt a hard kick in my stomach and wanted to reach a hand down to cradle it, but my hand wouldn't move. The twin Marissas cackled viciously, then turned into triplets wearing witch outfits with green faces like Elphaba Thropp. *Very weird.*

The three witches held up an hourglass, pointing to the sand. One witch screeched, "Time is running out for you and your twins, dearie!" They all glanced at one another and began cackling loudly, seeming delighted about my timely demise.

I began to panic. Up until now, even though the glue existed, I was able to breathe and still felt mostly normal. Now, my breaths were short, my blue eyes protruded and rolled around their sockets, looking down toward Leavensport. Another shock hit me that should have sent me slamming back against the branch of the tree, but the gunk held me in place as my body vibrated instead.

A voice yelled, "CLEAR!" Another shock of vibrations reverberated through my body; I heard the cackle of the three witches. I turned to them, and one morphed into Star, who whipped her long, black-painted fingernails around, scattering stardust in front of me and I saw a scene from my past.

Star standing at my door the day she came in and tried to kill me—calling me Barbie. My vision slowly drifted back down toward Leavensport where Earl Seevers sat in the middle of town in a chair that was large, golden, with jewels covering it—a throne. He wore the tight, skimpy leather shorts I had found him in with his wife Bea a few months back. He held a Barbie doll that resembled me in his hands, studying it. Suddenly, he snapped one of the legs off of the doll, and pain shot through my thigh.

"AUGHHHHHHHH!" I yelled into the paste that was slowly melting, turning more into the sugary blue mist I'd witnessed before. The sharp leg pain faded away as well, and then the witches were gone and my body floated toward the ground, toward Earl, who now wore his usual beige cardigan with jeans. Bobby Zane sat on his lap, wearing a red satin robe. The two men leered at me before a flash of lightning hit me, sending my spirit flying through space.

I sat upright, back in Madame Emerald's tent, sitting across from her again. The goblet was in my lap, and the caramel apple was still lying on the gold plate.

"What's happening to me, Great?" *Great-granny? Somehow, I was remembering the accident, my pregnancy, all the bizarre things that happened since the crash—it was all coming together--and I now knew this woman was related to me.*

"You are starting to see a bit more clearly now, my child. Listen carefully, we need to get you back to the physical world *before* your babies come into the world."

"Where am I?"

"You are in what's called the Betwixt & In-Between World right now as the doctors work to bring you back to life."

"I'm dead?!?" I gulped, rubbing my belly and feeling the twins kick.

"You are in between right now. Everyone down there thinks you are alive but in a coma."

"The girls!" I panicked.

"They're fine for now, but it's imperative I perform a spell to send you back." She pointed to the rusty golden goblet with the jewels shining through it. "I need you to go retrieve some water from the fountain by the casino in the tunnels. Then, I'll have everything I need to perform the spell."

"Granny, come with me," I begged her. "This is getting scary."

My great-grandma shook her head. "I wish I could, but I'm too weak. That casino is the heart of something dark. Going there would destroy me. But you can. And you must! Go now, child, and don't waste time!"

I took the goblet and closed my eyes tightly, visualizing the casino with its neon laser lights. When I opened them, I was back in the tunnel.

Now that's what I call not wasting any time! I thought to myself as I began to glide toward the fountain. I dipped the goblet into the water. It had changed to a thick substance that put off a sweet aroma. I dipped a finger in and rubbed my thumb and index fingers together. It felt like an oil, and I tasted it. That flavor was familiar—possibly the oil Mick used at his restaurant? I held the goblet near my stomach, protecting it to be sure I could get it back to my great-granny, Esme.

I felt something rush through me and jerked my head around like the girl in *Poltergeist*. The vampire was back. They were in the fountain, walking on the oil toward the entrance. The woman in the snake costume met them there. They turned to stare at me and pointed toward my stomach, eyes gleaming. Was the vampire going to approach me? Instinctively, I set the goblet down and wrapped my arms around my stomach, wanting to protect my girls.

The three statues in the fountain turned into the three witches and the casino took on the appearance of a large hourglass as the witches pointed, screeching loudly. The taste of the oil lingered on my tongue with an acidic bittersweet taste as a loud "AH—EH—AH—EH—AH—EH" sound surrounded me. I turned to see mummies walking toward me down the tunnel.

"Nina?" I called, shielding my eyes as a bright light blinded me. Time froze and I felt my spirit begin to center as an acrid smell filled my nostrils. I became confused at the extreme senses that had taken over the last few moments from the taste of the oil to the visions of these monsters and the blinding light, to the sounds of the mummies, the burning smell, and the touch of the—

"NO!" I yelled looking down and realizing the goblet was gone.

I felt a jolt to my body again, throwing me all the way back to Leavensport into the Cast Iron Creations kitchen. Emotions poured out of me, seeing my kitchen and the business I'd worked on creating since I was a child with my BFF Ava.

"Remember your roots, child, and never forget your Great loves you." Great-Granny Esme hovered next to me inside the restaurant.

"Granny, what's happening?" I asked as her body went from solid to spirit form. She transformed into her young, glorious, vibrant self, then shape-shifted into a beautiful eagle and spread her wings wide, flying over me and the entire village raining gold dust over the town.

Two tiny voices began calling out to me from somewhere far away. They felt familiar, like I should know them. They were female children. Alarmed, I hurried toward the voices.

"Mom. MOM! Help us, mom—wake up!" I looked up. The hourglass in the sky was steadily losing sand.

"GIRLS!?" I called out to my twins, trying to get to them but finding myself back in Great-Granny Esme's tent again. *I must be fighting something in the hospital* as I struggled to control where my spirit was.

"Jolie, the goblet?" Granny Esme asked as her lips thinned out like Grandma Opal, my mom, and me.

"It's gone!" I cried.

Granny Esme tilted her head toward the crystal ball, pointing to it as a scene from history unfolded inside. I saw my Granny Esme, who looked to be in her thirties. She sat in a tent similar to the one we were in now. Her head rested on the table where she last read my fortune—the table where we now sat. Beside her, the crystal ball was cracked and smudged with blood. My great-granny's eyes were open wide, looking off into space, and above them, there was a wound on her forehead. She was dead.

"Someone murdered you?" I wailed, turning back to the woman beside me. To my horror, my beautiful, long-haired granny began to change: her hair turned gray as her strong, youthful body withered, the flesh dwindling until she was a skeletal figure. She smiled woefully at me.

"I don't have much time now, Jolie." My granny's voice sounded weak. "Listen. You need to know two things about our ancestors' spirit world.

One is, that goblet belongs to our family. Only our relatives can see the jewels and understand the value of it. Find out who took it, retrieve it, bring it back to me with the oil in it, then rub the oil on my forehead so I can gain my energy back and perform the spell to get you back to your family."

"Great!" I yelled, watching her wither away to nothing but bones. "What's the second thing?"

"Dreamcatch-er ..." She tried to continue talking, but her eyes fluttered and closed.

"Great Esme!" I looked around, wanting to call out for help—but who do you call in the spirit world? I felt disoriented. A wave of panic surged over me.

The cool air became hot and smothering as I found myself in the tunnels underground. There was only pitch darkness, but suddenly flames burst out around me. A shadowy figure walked through the fire with the same joker grin the vampire displayed on the park bench. They held a crystal ball out to me, and inside, I saw myself in a hospital bed with family, friends, and husband all around me, gathered, holding hands in a circle. Then the ball turned black and I heard someone yell, "We're losing her!" and I was pulled back to the hospital room again, hovering helplessly near the ceiling, staring at the flat line on my heart monitor screen as a team of medics rushed around my body.

Chapter Six

Darkness surrounded me. I was a wailing newborn. Great-Granny Esme held me in her arms, but her long hair was charcoal gray and brittle and her face was skeletal. Her flesh had disappeared except for her beautiful dark eyes and blood-red lips. I could feel her bony hands and arms holding me. *Was I dreaming? In a different spirit world? Dead? I thought I had all this figured out!*

"Go back, child," she commanded.

I grew into an adolescent, pushing toward a light through a tunnel of a thick, sticky lavender material. It was exhausting, but I was able to struggle steadily toward the light. Three neon green faces popped out of the lavender goo, cackling at my expense. The three witches hovered together. They were playing the ultramodern slot machines from the casino. An hourglass floated over them.

"Where's the golden goblet?" I yelled through

the goo.

One of the witches said, "You mean that filthy hunk of rust? You do need to get back to your world. Your eyesight is playing tricks on you, dearie!"

Even in my dizzying dream, my PI instincts had kicked in and I had begun to suspect that the three witches were someone I knew, maybe someone in my family, and maybe they'd know where I could find the goblet, but they seemed to be people I didn't know. Still, I wasn't sure if this made them suspects or if it cleared them. Great-Granny Esme had said only our relatives would see the goblet for what it was.

I slowly turned back. My skeletal granny was growing translucent, but she stood with palms out and eyes closed, as though willing me to continue my forward journey.

"Great," I called to her, "who killed you?"

"This is your test, child. Continue the journey to save the people of the village from the monster's mouth—in doing so, you can possibly save the city too."

I reached toward her, wanting to climb back into her arms.

"No, Jolie—turn and go forward," Great Esme said.

I felt my head turn and I felt the coolness of sheets. My Grandma Opal was chanting something under her breath, standing over my hospital bed with the rest of my family and friends encircling me. I seemed to be going in and out of consciousness, but I couldn't tell if my family knew I could see and hear them at times. I tried to speak to them, just in case some essence of my message got through.

"I'm back, guys," I said loudly, trying to project my voice into this reality. "Thank you all for rallying around us. We're going to be fine. Ava, listen, I have a lot of information we need to add to our I Spy Slides—AVA!" I clapped at her face, then realized I was more conscious, more in this reality than I had been in a while. How could I figure out what the date was? I scanned the room for a calendar or any sign of how much time had passed since the accident.

The accident! I remembered what happened with the three black kittens and the truck. Something about Nina and Asher and Nestle—but it was still a bit foggy—this was good news and made me more determined to find this goblet!

I closed my eyes to rest a bit and gather my thoughts.

Great-Granny Esme said I needed to locate the goblet and only a relative can see the worth of it. When I retrieved the oil who all was there that could have taken it?

- *The vampire.*
- *The snake lady.*
- *The three witches.*
- *A group of mummies.*

It had to be one of them. But I'd just seen the witches and they didn't see the worth in it—unless they were lying to me.

Great Granny had mentioned a dreamcatcher and she'd chanted and done a tribal dance earlier—she'd mentioned the Cherokee nation.

I wasn't sure if I was conscious in the hospital now and dreaming or if this was a realm of the Betwixt & In-Between World, but the hourglass that had continued to show itself in the sky turned to a dreamcatcher with an eagle feather dangling from the side of it and a heart in the center that seemed to be beating. Colorful beads were locked within the web surrounding the heart in the center of the web. A seven-pointed star surrounded the circular web and laurel branches framed the beads within it.

Within this realm or dream I was in, I studied the dreamcatcher. *Symbolism. Laurel branches mean peace and I'll take an educated guess that the heart in the center represents matters of the heart. I know a bit about dreamcatchers. I've always loved them and had them in my home. The web represents the interconnectedness of life but that is also where the dreams were caught—like me—caught in-between right now. The circle within the star could signify the circle of life. The colors of the stones within the web were the same colors as the seven points of the star outside the circle. Maybe it represents something in the Cherokee culture? Different groups within the Cherokee nation? I have no clue what those groups or their responsibilities are, though. That eagle feather—Great-Granny had turned into an eagle that flew over the village—that feather was on the outside of the circle yet still attached to it—the web is connecting life—maybe the feather was some sort of connection between life and death?*

Right now, it was all speculation. I wished I could bounce ideas off of Ava so we could solve this mystery together.

While my eyes were closed, I decided to see if I could travel by focusing on the place I wanted to be most at that moment. I concentrated hard and opened my eyes to find myself lying in my bed while Mick sat at the side of it. I'd just seen him at my bedside in the hospital, so I had a feeling my mind was imagining him with me—that I needed to feel his presence in our bedroom at home. The fact I could will myself there made me think I was still in the Betwixt & In-Between World.

I saw my journal lying on the bedside table and I willed it to open to the last page I'd written on. I reread the last things I'd written.

Politicians, judges, lawyers, real estate/urban sprawl, jewelers, reporters, shelters/gentrification, pirates/gold, undercover agents, history–prohibition–tunnels.

It seemed like a list that covered the last few years since Mick moved to town and crime had started to pop up everywhere, starting with Ellie Siler's murder.

I willed myself to scribble down with my finger,

Great-Granny Esme Emerald——Cherokee——gypsy——
psychic——casinos. Wow, it worked! I was still
somewhere in between the worlds.

I looked up from the journal and found myself
back in the tunnels, but this time I could see
through to the ground above. I could see the mall,
completely built. I had to be in the future this time.

Marissa and one of the Zimmerman brothers
were standing in the parking lot. He shoved a stack
of cash into her hand. For some reason, it felt like a
scene I had watched before.

My body stiffened and dread rose in my chest
as I felt heat build up all around. The vampire
appeared, staring at me. The eyes were dark, cold,
wild, and the face was painted pasty white. It had a
drawn-on smile outlined in black with blood-red
painted lips, and the corners of its odd mouth
curved skyward. Then the mouth opened, revealing
teeth and tongue as it unleashed a horrid, deep
laugh. Everything became still around us and my
body was paralyzed.

My eyes could still move, but there was only
blackness—blackness and the creepy joker smile on
that white vampire face and the big red circles
under the dark eyes that bored into me. For a split
second, though, the eyes glinted light blue and
crinkled kindly at the edges. Could this be a clue as
to who this vampire who seemed to be the leader of
all the chaos was? Only the eyes smiled—the foul,
slick, painted mouth kept its devious sneer. The gray

hair turned dark green as the figure pulled a hooded black cape over their head, hiding the changing form. The being floated further back from me and I couldn't move toward it.

The cackle in the distance let me know the witches had found me and were closing in. The vampire roared out a thunderous laugh.

"Who are you? Did you murder my great-granny?" I yelled down the tunnel.

More cackling from the witches. The vampire let out another laugh that cut right through me, then lapsed back into silence. It pointed to me, then to itself.

I was confused. "I'm not you!" I yelled.

It laughed again, even louder, then a jolt of pain doubled me over, making me feel like I'd been kicked in the belly. Unexpectedly, Mayor Cardinal from Tri-City, Mayor Nalini, and Aunt Fern appeared, standing behind the vampire. Leavensport's local lawyer, Niko Mercurio, and others I recognized as city lawyers gathered and men and women in judge's robes approached, clustering around. A Nestle Construction truck drove down the tunnel, honking, and the vampire sat in the driver's seat, waving as the truck slowly passed me by.

As it passed me, I yelled again, "I'm NOTHING like you!"

The beeping sound came back louder than I'd heard it thus far. Maybe this meant I was getting stronger and was on my way back to my family. I caressed my stomach, feeling the twins kick. I heard their distant cries, begging me to come back. "Hold on, my little rug rats." I rubbed my stomach, more determined to figure out who had the goblet and how to get back.

I heard Bobby Zane's voice and opened my eyes. I was still my immaterial self, but I was in the hospital room. He was the only one there—the eyes of my physical form were still closed on the bed.

I crossed my arms, feeling a surge of hostility, and noticed my hovering body was wearing my pumpkin-and-cobweb-patterned maternity dress, and the white dress I first sported in the Betwixt & In-Between World was gone. I seemed to be slowly coming back to reality—more reason to find this goblet ASAP.

Chapter Seven

"I guess we will see how much your relationship to Ava means to you and your little happy-go-lucky Aunt Fern once she tries her hand at politics with the big boys."

The last time I saw this guy, he was sweating and shaking on my couch at the mere mention of the mob. Maybe he's gotten in good with them since then. Maybe he's on the inside now, instead of being their errand boy. Hmm. I don't like that at all. I stared daggers into Bobby Zane's head, feeling heat rise within me.

"Child, stop." I felt a breeze as Granny Esme hissed at me from beyond the spiritual plane.

"I'm not sure how much longer you and Ava will own your little cast iron restaurant, either. Not long enough to pass down to the little brats you're carrying around. I have no doubt they'll be as nosy as their parents."

I felt my face flush with heat and flames danced around my eyes as a burning darkness rose within me. Memories of my past as well as thoughts of all the broken children harmed by a parent rushed through me as my body burst into uncontrollable flames of fire. A strong, strange desire surged up, stretching out to take hold of the power I felt, ready to wield it against this man who threatened my family.

"Choices, Jolie," I heard from outside the flames. I assumed it was Great-Granny, but when I turned, I saw the familiar beard, large belly in bib overalls, and the jovial grin that my real-to-me dad, Mike, always wore. His expression made me wonder if he was up to no good or just being his normal goofy self.

My body cooled down and I rushed to him, feeling my eyes mist up. "How are you?"

"How I am is no longer relevant—but it still applies to you where you are—so, how are you?" he said in his therapeutic way. He'd wanted to study psychology in college but didn't have the funds to continue so he quit school to work for the phone company. He used his local library to give him all the education he needed for under five bucks in late fees—one of many reasons I loved him.

"I don't know how I am. I'm here—wherever here is—trying to figure out what happened to me in that world." I pointed to the me lying in the bed. "Plus, I'm getting all these cryptic messages about the future and I have no clue if I'll remember any of it IF I make it back to my family and friends. If I don't, then I guess I'll end up with you."

"Things aren't always so black and white," Mike said, shifting from the form I knew to more of an alien, fluid shape that seemed to be leaking yet never losing fluid—a genderless form. "You and Ava—as chaotic as you both can be together; your role, your calling, is to be peacemakers."

I laughed out loud. Us? The bicker sisters? Peacemakers? I had watched Ava tell off more people than I could count, and tell me off even more times than that. Then a realization washed over me as I thought back to what Granny Esme had said about saving the village and the city from the monsters. I would do anything for my village. "Really?" I cried out.

"It's the truth. It all comes down to your choices and your intentions behind those choices— don't ever forget that."

"You know," I said to him, "for someone who has no blood relation to me, I feel closer to you than I do most in my family."

Mike came back in his old Earth form for a fleeting second and a calm, happy warmth rushed through me. He opened his arms and I ran into his bear hug, feeling completely safe and secure again for a fleeting second—*I wish this feeling could be my eternity.*

"It can't be—I can tell you that much," he whispered against my hair. "Blood and family do matter—ancestry is a strong bond—sisterhood can change some women for better and some for worse. Light and darkness—it all exists in all planes."

My reality was warping and changing again and I couldn't tell if I was gaining consciousness or not. I scanned the hospital room but Bobby was long gone and it was as dark as the night sky outside the window.

As before, I attempted to will myself back to my bedroom and found myself there. *Well, that answers that. Can't teleport in the real world, so still ... wherever this is.* I decided that while I was there I could write some notes in my journal with my finger.

Ancestry, Madame Esme Emerald, Vampires draining life, blood, energy out of people equates to those in power for anyone that sits below the throne—ancestry—blue eyes.

If I made it back to my world, I hoped I remembered to investigate DNA and ancestry.

I wasn't sure I'd figure out who killed Granny Esme while in the Betwixt & In-Between World, but I hoped I could later read this entry to remind me to revisit the cold case once I was back to my life. But first, I needed to find the goblet and the oil. And fast! I didn't know what would happen if Granny Esme couldn't send me back before the twins arrived, but my guess was it wasn't good.

"Well, well, well, child look at you!" chirped a singsong voice.

"Ellie Siler?" I squealed, wishing Betsy and my grandma were here with me now. They would love to see her.

"In the—well—the," she glanced down at herself, recognizing her ethereal qualities.

"Altered state," I helped her, knowing she wanted to say 'flesh'.

"Yes, let's use that phrase. How's your grandmother doing? Tell me everything! Although, I already know that horny Tom Costello tried to get his hooks into her. That man's always been on the naughty side—although, knowing Opal—that's why she was attracted to him to begin with."

TMI! my brain screamed as I shook my head free of any visuals. "She's doing fine—spunky and sassy as ever."

Ellie's sweet giggle bubbled over and infected me, causing me to laugh for the first time since all this started.

"We've all missed you so much! Especially Grandma, she's lost without you!" I said. "Do you know anything about my family's past? Were there Native Americans in our family?"

"Oh yes! Cherokee! You mean to tell me you've never seen that in your grandma?"

"I never thought of it, I guess. Do you know anything about a golden goblet or what a dreamcatcher did in Cherokee culture?" I was grasping at straws at this point.

"Your grandma told me the story of your great-

great-great-granny, who was a Ghigau," Ellie began.

"A what?"

"A Ghigau was the most prestigious title a Cherokee woman could be given. It meant she was a war woman. I remember your grandma telling me that meant the Great Spirit would speak to her great-grandma—at least that's the story her mother told her. But something horrible happened to your great-great-great-granny and her life was taken too soon. It caused an uproar in your family's history, so her daughter, your great-granny, fought because of it, for the sake of your family. Your family turned on each other. That golden goblet divided them—it's worth a lot of money and money always equals power."

"Not in the spirit world, though," I said.

"Value and power exist in all the worlds—good and evil still exist—just in a different way that you can't understand until you are here. Anyhoo, that's one thing your grandma always regretted. Someone in your family has that goblet—in the physical world, and whoever it is—there's bad blood between your grandma and that person. Anger is like a disease. It gets passed down from one generation to the next. Think about the difficulties between your grandma and your uncles, for example. It's like poison."

Wow! I wonder why my grandma never told me about this part of our family history, I wondered to myself, forgetting Ellie could read my thoughts if she wished.

"It's painful for her to remember. But I digress. I've so loved watching you and Mick develop your relationship and build this beautiful home together." Ellie gestured with ghostly arms at the space around her. "Hey," she paused. "Would you mind passing a message on to my Betsy, please?" Ellie reached, then remembered she couldn't physically hold my hand.

I guessed a certain amount of energy had to be spent each time, so the spirits had to weigh out whether to use it or not. This extra energetic cost gave Mike and Granny Esme's hugs even more emotional value. "I'll do my best. I'm not sure how this will turn out, but if I get back and still remember this, you know I will." I smiled.

"Just tell her how proud I am of her and all she's sacrificed and done to take over my business. She's brilliant in the choices she makes for marketing."

I nodded my head, holding back tears, determined to make it back to relay the message to Betsy.

"Also, I chose not to touch you so I could save my energy. There are other things afoot here. This world and the world of the living are interconnected. Events that happen here influence what happens there, and things that happened there define things here. Even things that happened long ago." Ellie's brow furrowed and she gazed off into the distance. "Now you know we aren't allowed to reveal too much to someone like you, someone who might go back. It might fiddle with cause and effect." Ellie glanced around cautiously. "But please, go back and reinvestigate my death. Take a second look at who the real target was and why. Jolie, you recently found out your Aunt Fern was in dangerrrrr—" Ellie's spirit began spinning in circles as it got smaller and smaller and she yelled out, "Don't worry, dearie, I'm fine—I told a bit too much but no worriiiiiiiiiiies—" and she was gone.

Chapter Eight

Ellie's story about my ancestry gave me an idea. I willed myself to enter Cast Iron Creations to see how the business was going—and do a bit of snooping. Maybe there would be a clue as to where the goblet was, or what kind of oil was inside of it. I knew time was running out for my babies and myself.

Just like that, I found myself in the restaurant. I was getting better at maneuvering. I had figured out how to concentrate, kind of aim my mind and then...I don't know...sort of...*flex my brain* at where I wanted to be. I'm guessing a truly spiritual person would have terms for all of this. Not me.

Ryder Chen was in the kitchen, making what appeared to be pumpkin muffins in the shape of pumpkins with streusel on top, which was adorable. He paused and pulled cookies resembling witches' fingers out of the oven and moved them to the cooling rack with a satisfied smile. Nearby were some mummified blueberry muffins. *Man, I hope he wrote down those recipes!* I found myself thinking, despite my existential crisis.

I was having a hard time figuring out how time worked in this Betwixt & In-Between World I'd entered, but from the skeleton onesie Ryder was wearing plus an apron that showed an actual beating heart, I assumed it had to be Halloween morning. *This guy might have me beat for flair.*

I floated around the kitchen, being careful not to bump into Ryder—even though there was a good chance he'd never know. I hovered by the cabinet that held my grandma's cast-iron skillets. Three of them were over one hundred years old and I remember Grandma Opal telling me they belonged to her grandmother. I willed the cabinet to open and began pushing aside the skillets that were newer that I used daily to get to the older ones I'd placed in the back for safe keeping.

As I pushed the many sizes of cast iron pans to the side, I found the ones my grandma had wrapped in cotton pan covers. I gasped. The fabric was patterned with dreamcatchers that reminded me of the one I'd seen in the sky! I willed the cover off of the pan. I hovered, tilting my head, studying the old skillet. I could see bumps on the sides of the deep pan—where the pour spouts to release grease were located. I leaned in, tipping my chin lower to get a closer look. In my ethereal form, I could see through a thick coat of black paint and beneath that, a layer of clay covering and smoothing out the surface, making it appear to be a regular skillet handle. Under those two materials, the handle was made of large red rubies! I'd always thought the feeling of the handles and the spouts was odd compared to modern-day skillets. This hidden treasure would be concealed from the—er—*mortal eye.* I now understood why I was told not to use these pans and to keep them safe.

Ryder, unaware of my presence, continued cooking and swaying to the beat of Stevie Wonder's song, *Superstition.* I noticed he'd added a bloody vampire bite mark to his neck. My eyes slid down to the beating heart on his apron. *Matters of the heart. Family—jeweled goblet.*

I overheard a familiar voice in the dining area and hurried through the swinging kitchen doors to our quaint dining area, where Halloween themed decorations sat on each table and mummies, vampires, witches, and ghosts decorated the front window as a mural—thanks to Ava's wife, Delilah, Leavensport's own resident artist.

Tabitha, my therapist-slash-occasional-PI-colleague-slash friend, sat across the table from Marissa, a cup of hot tea in front of her. "That's an interesting dream, Marissa."

"I know—it's weird. I've been researching my family lately—but I keep having these dreams that a vampire is biting my neck. I wake up in a complete state of panic. I figured maybe you'd know how to interpret it?" Marissa fumbled with her hands, showing her discomfort in admitting weakness to anyone.

"Well, it could mean many things—or nothing at all. The fact you continue to have a reoccurring dream—some Freudian psychiatrists would tell you it signifies you are worried that you or a loved one is in danger—or illness is coming into your family. But many others would just as quickly dispute that. That unconscious part of our brains is difficult to pinpoint." Tabitha took a sip of her tea.

Jeweled family goblet, jeweled family skillets, dreamcatchers, vampires symbolizing draining blood and energy from people—only family knows there are jewels within our history—beating hearts within a web that connects the physical world and the spiritual world. Someone doesn't want me returning to the physical world. The same someone who stole the goblet ... and they are connected to, or maybe are the person who killed Great-Granny. The witches—while creepy—are helping me watch the time.

As I continued to ponder the clues I'd come across, I began feeling more present in my earthly world than the spirit side. I sensed that I had a choice of which I wanted to remain in. It seemed obvious—going back to my family to live my life was what I needed to do...but I was enjoying having powers I'd never known had existed—being able to mind-bend was super cool!

Then my stomach plunged as the realization struck me. *Ryder's costume—the snacks he was making, the decorations on the tables and the window—Halloween!* The twins were due soon. Very soon. I was running out of time.

I was learning that my...spirit guidance system...was sensitive to my emotions. I could steer to some degree when I stayed calm and focused, but panic sent me spinning off to another time and place.

I shook my head and realized I was back in my hospital room.

While I continued to try and figure out how to get the goblet back, I decided to do so in my hospital room as it helped me realize how loved I was in the community. Many members of the village came to visit me and rally the twins and me on. I'd stayed long enough to find out the babies were doing well—I was the problem. The spirit of Nina Sanchez wandered the halls of the hospital, eating her baked treats. She ignored me any time I tried to speak to her. I assumed she was trying to figure out this new world too—although from what I understood, she didn't have the same opportunity as me to return.

Bea Seevers had visited me the last few days since the accident, whispering encouraging words to me and the twins. I knew she and I shared a strong bond, but it was amazing to me to see that, outside of my family and closest friends, Bea was the only other one who showed up daily. Somehow, I was beginning to understand how time was moving here, in this world.

After learning what Granny Esme and Ellie had

shared about energy in the spirit world and the goblet's history in our family—as well as finding secrets hidden inside the old family skillets, I realized I needed to further investigate who took the goblet in the Betwixt & In-Between World or I may never get back to Mick. When I mentioned the goblet to the witches, they didn't seem to understand the worth of it. While they seemed creepy and their laughs were unnerving, they seemed to be more helpful than not, helping me keep track of time to get back to my world.

I heard the flapping of fabric and floated in front of a mummified Nina, who was eating a large snickerdoodle.

"Nina, STOP!" I grabbed a loose flapping rag and pulled on it, causing some of it to unravel as parts of Nina began to crumble into dust.

"Don't do that!" she squealed, reaching for the rags and rewrapping them as what had been dust turned back to preserved body limbs.

"I wouldn't have to if you'd talk to me!" I yelled back.

"Walk with me," she said, holding out one arm while doing a stiff walk and continuing to eat a never-ending cookie with the other. I could think of worse afterlives than being destined to spend eternity eating sweet baked goods. Hopefully, the preserved mummy body couldn't gain weight.

"Since I died ... I can't seem to stand still," Nina said. "And what kind of shoes are *those*?" She pointed to my orange and black Birkie clogs. Ava had made fun of me for pinning pumpkins on the buckles of the clogs, but I thought it looked cute.

Whoa, that's the first time I'd seen shoes on me since before the crash.

"Oh, I'm sorry." I clopped along with her, thinking about how best to approach the topic of Luis. "So, um, do you remember your life back there?"

"Yeah." Her voice softened, then she took a large bite of cookie.

"Were you married to Theo?" I asked.

"WHAT?!?" Nina finally stopped walking as cookie crumbs fell from her open mouth. "Of course not. That's disgusting!"

I was so confused. "I mean, how do you have his last name and Luis—he looks so much like him—and—" I stammered.

"Jolie, I lied. I'm Theo's sister," she said, beginning to pace the hallways of the hospital again.

"His sister!" I exclaimed, rushing to keep up with her.

"Jolie, one thing I've learned while here, I'm only allowed to say so much. This world is connected to the physical world, and, like an echo that bounces back and forth, they affect each other. The mummies that are following me—they are people from different mafia all over the world, they were double-crossed and murdered, so now they wander here, trying to find peace. The person who killed Esme and stole her goblet in the physical world created an echo here in this world too. Whoever has the goblet in this world took Esme's power in this world too—but there is a connection that is an echo from the real world. Someone in your family still has the goblet today—in the physical world—it's—

AHHHHHHHHHHHHHHHHHHHHHHHHHHHHHHHHHHHHHHHHHHH HHHHHHHHHhhhhhhhhhhhhhhhhhhhhhhhhhhhhhhhhhhhhhhhhhhhhhhhh hhhhhhhhhhhhhhhhhh!!"

The hospital floor opened up and Nina's mummified body fell into a dark abyss. A piece of her rag had caught onto the pumpkin pin that was hooked on the buckle of my clogs. I lifted my foot and then slammed it down on the floor, pinning the rag under my foot. Nina's left arm pulled out of her wrappings and instantly turned to dust, but she used her tattered-rag-covered right hand to hold onto the fabric that I was stepping on and hung there, looking terrified.

"I could use some help here!" I called out to the spirit gods.

"Ah-Eh—Ah-EH!" I heard the chant getting closer and cocked my head to the left to see an army of mummies coming toward me.

A spine-tingling sensation overtook me as I wondered if they were coming for my brains or to save Nina. Luckily, it was the latter. The mummies created a line as one of them removed the rag from my pumpkin pin. That mummy glanced up and smiled. "Tell Mick Papa Giuseppe said hi and kiss those girls for me." The mummy's voice was low and raspy and he winked at me with one of his brown eyes as he pointed to my stomach.

"Do any of you know anything about the golden goblet that I had when I was at the fountain?" I asked Papa Giuseppe.

"Rusty cups don't do anything for us," Papa said, gently moving me aside. "We'll take care of Nina from here."

They eased her up out of the dark pit and then turned en masse, marching down the hall toward the stairs with her safe among them. I saw her lift her right hand to her mouth to take a bite of her eternal cookie. Suddenly, a group of three mummies broke off, turned back to me, and wordlessly pushed me back into my hospital room. I looked over my shoulder as they disappeared. *That was...unnerving.*

Boy, do I have an earful for Bounty-Full and PURL if I can ever wake up from this! My only fear was not remembering what I'd learned and been told to find out about once I got back—I didn't know how all this worked—I didn't even know this realm existed—for all I knew, I'd awaken from the coma and never remember one thing about this time. THAT truly terrified me the most. I needed to explore my ancestry further and I didn't want to lose my memories of Great-Granny Esme. I needed to keep her spirit alive in me.

I heard something outside of my hospital room

and walked toward the soothing, low, melodic voices. Baggy and Myrtle, Leavensport's two people both vying for town troubadour, were not warring with each other for once; instead, they stood near one another. Baggy played the sax, and Myrtle took a deep breath and began to croon.

I Put a Spell on You,

Because you are mine.

I remember telling Baggy a few days before the accident that I loved that song and had to listen to it about twenty times every Halloween. I'm an odd duck in that Halloween is my favorite holiday of them all—hence humming Monster Mash to help calm me the morning of the accident.

I hovered, enjoying the contralto notes coming from Myrtle with the oscillatory vibrations of the sax playing in the background. Suddenly, I saw Marissa and one of the Zimmerman brothers talking as they walked down the hall. They stepped into the hospital elevator and the door slid shut.

I pushed my immaterial head through the elevator door to overhear their conversation.

"Child, that is a no-no of the realm where you currently reside," said Great-Granny Esme's voice in my ear. I glanced around but couldn't see her.

"But other spirits have shared things with me," I whined. "It's obvious they overheard and were monitoring what's going on there."

"They're in a different realm than you—they aren't coming back—you still could. If you change things here, it influences things too much…it sets what *is* in stone. It changes what *could* be. Don't risk it, child."

"Here, Zed," Marissa said. *At least now I know which Zimmerman he is,* I thought. I hoped I would be better at telling my own kids apart. *Wow, this may be why she's having those nightmares about vampires.* The two exchanged money and it reminded me of something I had seen in this world but I didn't know why. Everything in me wanted to stay in this realm and scout around, listening to everyone to see if I could figure out who was behind all of this, but I couldn't just think of myself now. I was carrying twins and I didn't want to jeopardize their lives, so I glided back to my room.

The witches continued to bother me—they confused me. There were three of them so of course, they reminded me of my mom, my grandma, and my Aunt Fern. But two of them took the forms of Bonnie and Star, two not-so-great women from the past. Yet that was inside the casino and the energy felt different when I was in there. Any other time I saw the witches, while they looked creepy and sounded horrifying, everything they did was helpful. They were showing me the hourglass and helping me keep time to get back. In the Betwixt & In-Between World, I realized the senses and intuition were as important as the conscious and subconscious brain were in the natural world. My intuition was practically yelling that I could cross the witches off the list of suspects. Nina clarified who she had been in the physical world and who the gang of mummies were and they had zero desire for the goblet—that left the snake lady and the vampire.

Chapter Nine

I wasn't aware I could fall asleep in the spiritual world until I woke up and found myself back in my bedroom where Mick lay napping.

I smiled and began drifting toward him when a long-legged, pouty-lipped, Italian beauty with dark curly hair appeared, lying at his side. My rage burned so hotly that I saw wisps of smoke forming around my ankles.

"Imelda," I growled, "what are you doing here? Don't tell me my greatest wish has been granted and you've been shanked in prison and are now here in the spirit world." I know—mean of me—but I wasn't myself with this witch. I was beginning to understand all of the fire and ice metaphors from the books I'd read over my lifetime.

"This must be a dream your simple mind has conjured up because I'm alive and well—you'll soon find out how well," she purred, tracing my husband's shoulder with her long, manicured nails, moving slowly down to his hip and down his leg, grinning lasciviously at me.

"You don't realize it yet—dream or no dream, spirit world or not—I'll cut a bi—" I lunged toward her as flames flared up around me.

Imelda held up a well-manicured hand. My flames dissipated instantly and my body froze. She went from lying on my side of the bed to bending on her knees, leaning over and kissing Mick on his cheek—then, she glanced over her shoulder with narrowed eyes just to make sure I caught it.

I willed myself to move but to no avail.

"Yooooooou are sssssssssssooooou predictable," Imelda transformed into a long, sleek, scaly serpent that undulated toward me, slithering up around my legs to my torso, gliding her head in front of mine as she squeezed my body.

Her head changed back to human form while her body remained a snake, continuing to constrict my paralyzed figure. "You do realize even IF you survive this, you and those little imps living in your stomach—" Imelda made a point to squeeze my midriff tighter, "—won't survive for much longer. Why prolong it? Let go. Be free to be with Mike and find out more about your Great-Granny Esme. I promise to take care of Mick for you." A devilish grin split her face, teeth gleaming in the flickering lamplight.

I couldn't move, but I had an idea. I wondered if she would take the bait. I suspected I would be "spending" a huge chunk of my spiritual energy to do this, but it might be well worth it. I stared at the water glass on my bedside table, overlaying it with my memory of the golden goblet, willing them to mesh. To my surprise, the water glass shimmered and transformed into a facsimile of the goblet. I felt exhausted, depleted, but I kept going. I gritted my teeth and used my mind to lift the goblet, making it hover over her head.

It didn't make sense that her or her ancestors would know my family and have anything to do with Great-Granny Esme's murder, but I needed to be absolutely sure while I had this opportunity as time was running out.

Imelda glanced up at the goblet in confusion. "What? Are you planning to hit me with tarnished trash?" She constricted my midriff tighter, grinning wickedly.

"MOM! HELP US! We can't breathe!" I felt my girls calling from deep within me.

"SSSSSSHHHHHhhhhhhhh, little ones—once you are gone, your mama will have nothing to live for." Imelda's slithering body jerked back as her head struck my midriff area and my girls shrieked in fear.

Something primal erupted in the depths of my soul. Behind my eyes, a nebula in the shape of a witch's head glowed in the dark part of my mind. The cloud went from gas and dust to a blazing fire as my eyes opened and flame roared in my irises and pupils. The coils of the snake loosened and I felt oxygen and sensation return as the snake's slithering body transformed into long, muscular legs and arms. Human again, Imelda tilted her head slowly left to right, cracking her neck in a menacing fashion. She nodded, somehow pleased, and stepped into a fighting stance.

"I tried to warn you." I spent a solid second considering whether to fight honorably or not. I saw a vision of a dreamcatcher. The heart in the center of the web was beating like a living human heart. *Fight honorably as your ancestors would have*, it seemed to say.

Why am I thinking like a Cherokee warrior?

My form took on a weight and silver armbands circled my wrists and continued up my arms. Startled, I checked my reflection in the window. I wore a long beaded panel over deerskin pants with a vest. A wool headdress decorated with rows of animal teeth appeared on my head and my body was painted blood red with black paint across my eyes. I held a tomahawk with an eagle feather attached to the base with a leather tie. A bow and arrow sat in the corner of the bedroom as Mick tossed and turned on the bed below us. I looked like a warrior.

A battle-ax appeared in my other hand, then reality shifted into something like an animated cartoon. Imelda took the form of a snake woman again—neon green scales covered part of her forehead, five-inch, thickly mascaraed eyelashes framed her emerald eyes, vibrant red and green lips pouted as multiple live snakes wrapped themselves around her green-and-blue-scaled body. Her previous appearance was creepy enough, but this was a new level of terror.

In the natural world, snakes were my greatest fear. The atmosphere around us rumbled, stretching out a long low growl of thunder, followed by a crack of lightning. Mick continued to sleep, unaware of the video game that was about to begin above his head. *Typical man.*

I gripped my tomahawk. *It's best to cut off the head of a snake. Wait. How do I know this?* I lunged at Imelda's throat.

She dodged easily to the right, a wicked glint reaching her roguish green eyes as a gleeful smile spread across her face. "I'm going to love being the one to kill you." Imelda's body rippled like an ocean wave, using the bed to push off toward me.

I spun around in a tribal war dance, feeling a chant rise within me—as I spun, I witnessed my long dark blonde curls grow longer and interlace into two braids that fell to my waist. When I saw Imelda pause to watch for my next direction with the dance, I launched a spinning kick, catching her in the gut. A split second later, two snakes wrapped around my leg. "AHHHHHHHH!" I shook my leg hard and they fell to the floor. Even Cherokee Warrior Jolie didn't like snakes.

Imelda hissed, then struck again. This time, I combined my ancestry and spiritual powers to hover straight up through the ceiling as she flailed into the wall. I felt I had to be dreaming this if she wasn't able to go through the wall. I came back toward her with the tomahawk in one hand and the battle-ax in the other and willed myself to gain as much speed as I could manage. I felt a war cry come from the depths of me as I raised my weapons—

"Child, NO!" my Great-Granny Esme yelled as she, Mike, Ellie, and Pria all stood in front of me, blocking me from Imelda.

My body slammed hard against an invisible barrier, the will of these spirits that I not take a life on this in between plane manifested as a brick-hard wall that brought me to a painful stop. I fell back, feeling confused as to where I was. Voices rose and I heard my mom cry out, "I can't do this anymore. I want her back NOW!" *Back in the hospital room.*

My body felt like a train was rolling over it. The world around me bounced and I tried to grab onto something, but my hands grasped emptiness. I felt sick to my stomach. Imelda was gone and I was flying through a rainbow of auras—neon greens, yellows, reds, purples. A blinding light filled my vision and a strong wind whipped my face as I tunneled straight down from the sky with no parachute and hit the ground—HARD.

Chapter Ten

I awakened surrounded by crumpled, rusting cars. I was in a junkyard. I assessed my body, as I had formed the habit of doing, to gauge how far off of normal I was. Things seemed…realistic. I panicked, wondering if I'd died, but then I realized my Honda CR-V was sitting in front of me. It looked like something huge had literally driven over the front of the car. The hood of the Honda was crumpled up against where the windshield used to be, and the front and roof of the vehicle were smashed, leaving little room where the impact had burst the seats out of the confines of the bolts that held them in place. The only thing that made it still resemble a vehicle was the busted, deformed tires. I stared in horror.

"There's no way I could have survived that," I muttered to no one, holding my stomach protectively. How could an accident like that occur in a village where the highest number on any speed limit sign was thirty-five?

Without warning or intention, my awareness was pulled back to my hospital room. I was startled, wondering if I'd entered another plane in the afterworld. Mick lay next to me in the hospital bed, resting his head on my belly, rubbing it with one hand as tears streamed down his face.

"I've been doing my damnedest to be strong, Jolie, but I have to be honest with you—I don't have much more in me. You've always acted like I'm the strong one since I'm older than you—wiser is what you said, but that's never been the truth." He sighed and readjusted, resting his head on my chest with an arm draped over me, holding my hand. "When I met you, you changed me. I am who I am now because of you. So, here I am again, asking you to be the strong one. Please come back to me—" He gulped and then sobbed on my shoulder.

I reached for him and laid a hand on his back, but I couldn't feel him. Helpless pain and despondence welled up in me. Next, I laid a hand on the round stomach of my own physical form. I felt a kick and jumped back—I had assumed I'd feel nothing after trying to touch Mick's shoulder. My little monsters were talking to me. I wondered if unborn babies were in some other plane as well?

"Mick." Dr. Delagada walked into my room and pulled a chair over next to the bed.

My husband tried to discreetly wipe his face on the sheet before turning over to sit up and speak to her. Guys are ridiculous when it comes to emotions—it was obvious from her facial expression that she knew he had been crying.

"My nurse told me she was concerned about you when she checked on you—your blood pressure was too high and she said you were struggling to speak at times."

"Well, my life isn't swell right now." He splayed his arms out to indicate the hospital room.

"I understand that. You still need to work on taking care of yourself while all this is going on."

"I'm doing the best I can." Mick rested his head in his hands.

"You've been having flare-ups more frequently the last six months—so much so that it affected your ability to walk. I'm trying to tell you—"

"I GET IT!" Mick exploded. "But listen. I need to be here for them. No matter what it does to my body. I'm sorry—if I end up in a wheelchair, then so be it!"

"Oh Mick," I whispered.

"Dr. Delagada," Lydia popped her head in. "Do you mind if I talk to Mick alone?"

She nodded, momentarily turning to nod at Mick, then heading out of the room.

"I'm imagining the look Jolie would give you for blowing up at your neurologist," Lydia said, taking a seat and rubbing my shoulder. She gazed at my body with anguish in her eyes, then changed it to resolve as she straightened her back and turned to address Mick.

"I know—I can only do so much," he

whimpered.

"Mick, things happen in life that we have no control over. And this, this is horrible—absolutely horrific." *Okay*…thus far I was underwhelmed by this pep talk. "But," she continued, "she and those twins are still alive and they are all fighting to come back to you. Don't you think they deserve to come back to the healthiest version of you?" Lydia stared Mick down with her hands on her hips and a bulldog expression on her face.

Mick chuckled softly. "I was just telling her she's always been stronger than me."

"Well, DUH! She's a woman—of COURSE she's stronger than you. That's not my point. It's what can you do to be ready for when they come back— because they *will come back to you*."

Mick seemed to be pondering that thought when Lydia stood up, then bent down and whispered to me, "You owe me one, witch." She grinned to herself and walked out.

Touché! A smile spread across my face. I was starting to adore the little love-hate relationship we had going on.

Chapter Eleven

I'd had about enough of this limbo state—
Halloween was here and the twins were due soon. I
hovered out of the hospital and glided around the
town. I saw out at the pond at the park they had the
huge, hollowed-out pumpkins ready for the
villagers to paddle across the water in them in their
costumes—a fun tradition I'd taken part in since I
was a little kid.

I popped in on Ryder in the Cast Iron Creations
kitchen and he was pulling out thirteen skull-
shaped cast iron cake pans—some chocolate, some
vanilla, some strawberry and some swirled. I saw
Ava was keeping my annual tradition of serving
skull-shaped cakes on Halloween alive.

Lydia was dressed as a "wolf in sheep's
clothing" with little Monty as the cuddly little
sheep. *That is slightly terrifying.* I couldn't help
but giggle at her dark humor, though. Baby Monty
was entering into a world of dysfunction—he might
as well get used to it young.

I drifted over and hovered directly above Monty. "Da ba ba da," he babbled, reaching for me.

"Hi, little dude, how are you doing? I'll get your tummy!" I tickled him and he giggled uncontrollably.

Between him and my twins, it seemed clear that babies haven't formed enough cynicism yet, so they can see into other planes.

"What are you laughing at, you silly boy?" Lydia asked him. "Mama will eat you up! You know I will, you little lamb!"

Loud, horrific bass drum booms shook my world and I tried to steady myself on Monty's stroller, but of course, my hand went right through it. He went from giggling to wailing in Lydia's ear as his little cheeks flushed red.

"It's okay, sweet boy, I'll take care of this," I promised, trying to figure out who was doing this.

An irritating, high-pitched clicking, like the sound of many bats, echoed throughout Leavensport, and only Monty and I seemed to be able to hear it. The squawk grew higher in pitch until only I could hear and I recognized that it was the sound of the green-faced witches from the spiritual plane. The sound seemed to be coming from down the interstate near the new mall that was under construction.

I hovered, squeezing my eyes shut and willing my Cherokee armor to reappear with the bow and arrow in my hand. I zoomed toward the mall, blazing past all the traffic on the highway. *Wish I could do this in the physical world.*

Upon arrival, I hovered and looked around. The mall had been completed. *This must be the future*, I thought to myself, always a bit confused where I was in time in this state. My grandma, Aunt Fern, and mom were dressed in their annual Macbeth witch costumes. All three women were staring at something or someone behind a wall of the newly built mall. I didn't know if I was in the next year or the year after—no one had given a firm date as to when the mall would open—the tentative plan was spring of 2023.

I swept forward through the air and saw the vampire with the cape pulled over their head. Neon green hair stuck out from the hood as the creepy white face looked up at me.

"I don't know who you are, but I know you or one of your ancestors murdered my great-granny. Are you somehow related to us?" I asked the vampire, realizing I'd crossed every other suspect off the list. I knew this beast had the goblet. *They must have been staring at the goblet and not my pregnant belly*, I realized, thinking back to the fountain when the goblet went missing.

"No, Jolie, go back!" my mom yelled at me.

"Mom, you can see me?" I yelled down to her and tried going toward the vampire, but the vampire froze me in mid-air just like Imelda had.

"You can't get to them, dearie," the predator hissed at me.

I gasped. The vampire had never spoken

before. I still couldn't tell if the voice was more feminine or masculine because it was distorted. *Dearie—more a term a woman would use?*

I willed myself to break free as I'd done with Imelda. I focused with all my strength, but nothing.

"Child, don't try with this one. You will use all the energy you have left," I heard Great-Granny Esme's voice whisper in my ear.

"Awwww, Esme Emerald—I thought I'd taken care of you once and for all," the warped voice rang out as I saw a youthful Esme take form.

"Don't, Great," I mumbled, not sure if what I said was coherent to her since even my lips were immobilized. She'd told me she wasn't strong enough to face the negative energy at the casino, and the vampire certainly seemed like a strong negative force also—I didn't know what could happen to her if she tried to rescue me.

My eyes were able to move around, and I could see the women in my family who continued to stare, terrified, at the vampire. They seemed to know who the creature was. I'd always thought of these women as strong, independent, unafraid—yet this thing had them petrified.

"There you are, my youthful beauty—always so pretty," the vampire's eyes turned red as they gazed ravenously over my Great-Granny's figure.

"And strong, don't forget strong," Great-Granny said, taking in a deep breath.

Great-Granny and I held a stare as she flicked

her eyes to the vampire's cape for a split second. I turned my blue eyes to see a glimpse of gold and jewels behind the cape.

I blinked twice. Hopefully, she could read my thoughts—if she could distract this beast, I could try to break free and retrieve the goblet to bring the oil to her.

"Not strong or smart enough to survive my descendants." The predator paused and tilted their head, turning those flaming eyes to each of the women in my family, Great Esme, to me, then to my middle. The vampire appeared, eye-level with my stomach which I felt grow two times larger. *What is this creature going to do to me?*

"CLICK—CLICK—CLICK—SQUEEEEAAAAALLLLL!" the vampire screeched in a booming voice that shook the world. "Every so often the teacher needs to learn from the pupil. And occasionally you need to plummet EXTREMELY far to finally see the illumination out of the darkness. Isn't that right, ladies?"

I felt the girls begin to kick in fear. Time was running out. Something primitive welled up in me, giving me strength.

My great-granny was now in a witch hat paired with a deerskin warrior dress and moccasins, making a fourth Macbeth-slash-Cherokee-warrior-witch sister. The vampire guarded me as Great-Granny flew toward them, catching the bow and arrow I'd thrown to her mid-air.

Fire rose in my eyes and I burst out of the vampire's powerful hold and sprinted away as Great-Granny Esme reared her strong body back, stopping suddenly, pulling back the arrow in the bow as her chiseled bronze arms gleamed with sweat. She aimed swiftly and released, sending the golden-jeweled arrow straight into the vampire's forehead.

Hundreds of bats descended from the sky upon us as the vampire continued its deafening "CLICK—SQUEEEAAAALLLLL!" although the vampire staggered, clutching their face. Then they regained their footing and pulled out the arrow, shaking their head as though to clear it from some small annoyance. They turned to me, winked, and cackled loudly. "You win this round, Esme! But the war is still not over!" Then they clapped four times and disappeared, along with my family and the bats. I fell to the ground with a loud THUMP. The goblet appeared in my lap. I reached inside and felt that the oil was still there.

I sat up, thinking about how hungry I was—this had to be the longest I'd ever gone without thinking about food, let alone eating it. The mall stood before me half-built, Nestle Construction trucks were parked in what would soon be a concrete jungle.

I saw Asher and Caleb jump out of a truck a few spaces down. They began walking down a tunnel formed by semis that were parked in the lot.

There was Nestle, waiting behind one of the looming tractor-trailers.

I stood and walked toward them, cautiously aware of gravel beneath my feet as to not make any noise. I peeked around the truck where they all lurked.

"Nice work, boys," I overheard Nestle say. He handed a thick stack of cash wrapped in a paper band to each man. "Whether she makes it or not, she won't be messing with us anymore."

"Child, I've warned you," Granny Esme said.

"I didn't do it on purpose!" I protested.

"MAMA! IT'S ALMOST TIME!" my girls yelled as I realized that's why I could hear the gravel below my feet. My body and spirit needed to get back to my world fast. I checked the hourglass in the sky and the sand was almost gone.

"We still aren't in your world yet. You may have been able to remember some or all of this when you go back—but now, I'm not so sure with your spying in the Betwixt and In-Between World. Your spirit form exists in all the realms—you are everywhere and nowhere in the universe. Come back to me now, child."

I willed myself back to the tent and rubbed the oil on my hands then rubbed my great-granny's skeletal forehead, moving to her cheeks then her neck, and down her breastbone to her heart, when the bones began to be replaced with flesh her body and face took on the middle-aged woman I'd first met when I entered the tent.

"Great-Granny." I reached for her as tears spilled over.

She put a hand up to stop me. "No, Jolie, I can't afford to lose any energy now. Lie on this cot and let all your thoughts go—become one with me and with nature in your mind's eye," she commanded while muttering a checklist of things she needed to perform the ceremony to get me back to my world—my family, my kids. "Mint tea, the oil, eagle feathers, and wild cherry bark."

I felt myself lying in a bed and twisting and turning as Granny Esme chanted, standing over me in the dark sky with the moon bright and stars shining around her. "Waya-hey-hey Waya-hey-hey Waya-hey-hey." She tipped the golden goblet, dripping oil on my head—the oil went from warm to cool on my forehead as I tasted a clean, crisp, warm mint flavor in my mouth. In my mind, the dark night shifted into colorful pastel fields, trees, and sky. My great-granny, fully adorned in her headdress, raised her hands to the sky and tossed the eagle feathers into the wind, then threw the wild cherry bark into the sky. The feathers transformed into a soaring eagle. I felt my spirit rise, sitting in a meditative pose as I began to deeply rumble the same chant—"Waya-hey-hey Waya hey hey ..."

She began a new chant. "Ancient moons, lend your power, to bring me peace this very hour. I call upon your strength and might to heal this child this very night." Her voice rose in volume and passion. *"Ancient moons, lend your power, to bring me peace this very hour. I call upon your strength and might to heal this child this very night!"* I felt the energy in my body shift and knew the spell had worked. I was going home.

She gazed at me with tears in her eyes, cupping my cheek. "Be well, my child. It's been an honor to know you. I'll always be with you!"

I gasped, feeling like I was rushing upward at an impossible speed. A flood gushed through my body and when it was gone, it was replaced by a wave of pain. Suddenly everything was cold and bright and loud.

"JOLIEEEEEEE!" screamed Ava. *Yeah, extremely loud.*

My body was a sea of agony. My head throbbed and my stomach felt like it was tearing itself apart.

"AVA?!!!!" I yelled—"OWWWWWWW WHAT IS HAPPENING TO ME?" This was the worst pain I'd experienced yet and nothing in the Betwixt & In-Between World compared to it. Then the pain released for a moment and I collapsed back on the pillow, gasping for air.

"You're back, baby, and you're in labor," Mick said as tears sprang from his eyes.

I looked around, bewildered, and saw Ava and I were in a large room. Her bed was several feet away from mine, and Delilah was there, holding Ava's hand. I turned to Mick, confused.

"She's in labor too. Of course, you two would manage to go into labor at the same time." Mick laughed.

"She refused to be in a separate room, so we moved you both into a double delivery room," Dr. Snyder sang out.

"GIRL IT'S ABOUT TIIIIIIIMEEEEE!" Ava yelled from her bed. Then her face scrunched up and she doubled over, moaning.

Just then, another contraction seized my body. "OH, GO HAVE A BABY!" I screamed back to vent my pain.

I guess not even a coma and labor phased us—we were right back to our verbally abusive selves.

Chapter Twelve

For the next twelve hours, I was in the worst pain of my life. I was exhausted, confused, and people kept taking my hand only to pull away from me as if I were a car compactor once I started squeezing. I think it was Mick who kept giving me ice chips. I couldn't stop sweating, and my curls were plastered to my face.

Ava and I found that yelling insults at one another when our contractions hit gave us an outlet. Mick and Delilah ranged from being amused to humiliated by our hours-long exchange.

"OWWWWWYOUR HAIR LOOKS LIKE SOMEONE ELECTROCUTED A MOP!"

"YYYEEEOOOOWWWELL YOUR CAR SMELLS LIKE A CAT FACTORY!"

Eventually, things progressed, and our obstetricians told us the babies would be here soon.

"We need one more BIG push, Jolie," Dr.

Snyder urged, echoing what my uterus was telling me.

"EEEEEAAAHHHHHHHHHHHHHHHHRRR RRRRRAAAAAAAAAAA!" I leaned my body up, eyes bulging, teeth gritted. I felt pressure, a big shift, and then a huge relief.

"WAAAA-WAAAA—EEE—EEE—WAAAA!" A shrill voice rang out. I sank back on the bed in relief but then felt another contraction and realized that the other twin was still waiting to arrive.

"Okay, little gal number two is ready!" sang the doctor. "One more push should do it!"

I flexed my body harder than I have in my entire life and then heard the second cry. My babies were here! We made it!

"I—need—to see—them," I said between gulps of air. I tried to sit up but my mangled abs refused. I wasn't quite sure what happened with the accident, but I knew I had just had the craziest dream. It was like one of those nightmares that seem so real ... I've had them before and couldn't shake them for hours after being awake. "Wait, Ava!?" I called, suddenly realizing I hadn't heard my friend wailing for what seemed like forever.

"I'm over here!" Ava called from her bed, holding their little girl to her bare chest. "We're all good! How are you doing, mama?"

"I want my girls," I cried out again, glaring at Lydia.

"Hold on, Jolie," Lydia blocked me and pushed

me back lightly. "The doctors are looking them over, then we'll get them right over here to you."

"Lydia, I am NOT kidding!" I wriggled against her arms, but I had little strength left.

"Jolie, calm down, girl," Ava called from a few feet away.

"Hey beautiful, let me see those baby blues." Mick reached for me, tears dripping from his chin, likely left over from when I was breaking his hand.

"Mick? What happened to me?"

"You were in an accident. You'd pulled over to the side of the road for some reason. Then, when you pulled back onto the road, you pulled in front of a construction truck."

"Asher," I said, remembering he was behind me at one point.

"Yeah, he tried to swerve to miss you but the truck had brake issues and was carrying a heavy load of blocks for the mall—he hit the side of the CR-V and then ran over the front—it sent both vehicles onto the sidewalk where Nina Sanchez was—she was hit and died on impact," Mick said rubbing my hand. "That was some scare you gave everyone!"

"Oh yeah, I'm starting to remember—I—" I began.

"You'd called us, Jolie," Delilah interrupted. "You were asking if the three girls got loose—it was a strange call—you sounded—off."

"Here we go!" Dr. Snyder interrupted with

Lydia at his side. "Everyone has ten fingers and ten little toes and they're doing great. Good job, mom!" Lydia reached down, helping me untie the hospital gown to expose my bare chest, then she and my OB each took a girl and laid them on me so our skin touched. Lydia laid a blanket over the twins to help keep them warm as we bonded.

Lydia pulled a curtain between Ava and me to give her and Delilah and Mick and me some privacy.

I laid back, feeling a relaxing warmth surge through me. Tears ran down my cheeks as I held my girls against me. We laid like that for over an hour as Mick sat, going between rubbing my arm and the girls' backs.

Lydia came back in, asking if she could help with diapers and an outfit, and we worked to get them clothed and blanketed. Hearing the cries of the girls and seeing them all bundled up in blankies as Mick held one and I the other in our arms was all too much—I completely lost it.

'Hey, it's okay—you're all okay and there could not be a happier man in the entire world." Mick reached over with one hand wrapping it around my head as I used my one free hand to wrap it around his neck and we kissed, cried, and laughed all at the same time.

It had been a hectic—wait... "What day is it?"

"Hey, girl, get it together—" Ava said as Lydia opened the curtain and Ava, with the baby in her arms, sat in a wheelchair as Delilah pushed her near my bed. "It's our favorite holiday, so of course our little Disney villains all knew they had to come today!"

"Ooooh, let me see!" I squealed, trying to sit up and failing. *Owww, my abs.*

"Jolie, you need to take it easy for a bit," said Lydia, taking one of the girls from me. "You suffered a head wound and were out of it for a good seventy-two hours."

"WHAT?!? Only a few days?" I yelled out, thinking about the dream I'd had and how time had played tricks on me.

"It felt a lot longer than that to us," Mick said.

Lydia smiled down at the baby she held. "Who is this one?"

I glanced at Mick and bit my lip. We had had several discussions over names but hadn't come to a definite decision yet and now I felt like the worst mother on Earth.

"Did you and Delilah decide on a name?" I asked Ava.

"We did. I think you're going to love it!" Ava squealed, gazing down at the cutie in her arms.

I was ready to hear *my* name come out of Ava's mouth when she declared, "Pria!"

I was taken aback momentarily that it wasn't my name, then a warmth rushed through me as tears welled up in my eyes. "Oh, that is JUST PERFECT!" I shrieked.

"Hey, you don't need to worry about it at this

exact second." Lydia waved my concern away. "Technically, you have up to six weeks to register your babies' names."

Ava almost rolled over Mick's toes to get to me as Lydia took both our girls and we reached for each other and held each other for a long, awkward amount of time. Neither of us cried, just hugged each other with our eyes squeezed shut. I thought about how fortunate I was to have her in my life.

"I missed you," Ava whispered to me. "Don't ever do that to me again!"

"Promise," I whispered back. "Now, get off me!"

"Girl, you wish!"

I laughed and it felt great to be back amongst the living. *Amongst the living . . . my dream felt so real.*

Images of golden goblets, blue-gray hair, babies, fortunes, Tarot cards, witches, snakes, and—

"Jolie," Mick said.

I looked up. "Yeah?"

"Well, what do you think we should name these little scamps? The last names we'd talked about were Julie and Jacey so they'd have J names like yours."

I didn't know why—but two names popped into my head that seemed perfect. "What do you think about Esme and Emerald?"

Chapter Thirteen

The doctors insisted I remain in the hospital for a few more days while they ran a ton of tests on me. They kept the girls as well to watch them. Since I was unconscious for over seventy-two hours, Dr. Snyder said he'd rather be on the safe side and Mick and I agreed. They ran a lot of neural tests on me because I'd been unconscious for so long. They told me that spending between six and seventy-two hours unconscious is considered to be a severe head injury and carrying twins made it all the more dangerous. I was sure I'd still owe my life in medical expenses even after insurance paid its portion. My mom always told me to be thankful I had insurance and while I knew she was right, I couldn't help but think about the debt that would be hanging over my head even after I recovered.

The next few days consisted of holding the girls as much as I was allowed, getting jabbed and prodded by doctors, and missing my usual Cast

Iron Creations food every time my meal arrived on a tray. The main attraction of my day was the girls. They were tiny, each weighing in at five point two pounds. They had delicate arms and legs and shell-pink skin, and their fingers and toes resembled miniature works of art. Mick and I learned how to position the pillows the best way to rest their tiny heads comfortably. I learned how to nurse and was already in love with them.

One week turned into two weeks of being in the hospital, when one afternoon, I was sitting in my hospital bed after Lydia had taken the girls for their nap, flipping through a cooking magazine, when three small black furballs flew past my open hospital door. I gasped. I reached for my portable IV pole and tried to jump out of bed. Bad idea!

"What . . . are . . . you . . . doing?" Lydia came through the door and rushed toward me, gently pushing me back on the bed before I fell forward. She gave me the death stare. "So, you clearly can't be trusted to not be a moron."

"I...saw...ahem...three black. Um. Kittens." I pointed to the door, realizing how ridiculous that sounded.

Lydia stared at me as her left eyebrow took the elevator to the top floor of her forehead. "We don't allow pets in here unless they are service pets, like Spy—but even they are only allowed in certain parts of the hospital. No kittens," she said firmly. "But sometimes the epidural can cause migraines and some women swear they see things when they get the headaches—not to mention you suffered a head injury." Lydia pulled the covers over me then reached into her bag and handed me my journal.

"How'd you get that?" I sat up too fast again. I didn't think I had a headache until I tried that move and a sharp stabbing pain arced across my skull.

"Calm down, Ava brought it in to give me this morning to give to you—so here!" Lydia held out the brown leather journal with a floral wreath etched on the cover.

I snatched it from her, holding it to my chest and thinking about wringing Ava's neck the next time I saw her.

"Don't worry, precious, I don't care what you write about me in there." Lydia gave me a wicked smile.

She wasn't wrong about some things I'd written about her in the past. "It's just like Ava to take something private and bring it out in public—why didn't she bring it herself?" I asked, realizing how rude my statement had just been. But I wasn't feeling great, I missed my girls and Mick, and I was frustrated.

"Oh, she said there was some catastrophe at Cast Iron Creations she had to handle. Delilah stayed with baby Pria while Ava went to figure it out. Pria has Ava's beautiful skin and gorgeous blue eyes—the contrast of her tan skin with those blue eyes is stunning—I want to eat her up!" Lydia squealed.

An image of Lydia in a sheep in a wolf's

costume with Monty as a lamb popped into my head.

"That's a weird expression," Lydia said and I realized my face must have gone funny. She handed me a few pens. *Thoughtful.* There was a good chance I'd want to journal while stuck here.

"I don't know—yeah—a strange thought," I said and waved it off.

Lydia pivoted toward the door. "Do you need anything before I head out?"

"Nope, I'm good other than when do I get to see the girls again?" I asked. My last visit was only an hour ago. The doctor wanted to monitor the twins too and he was dictating how often I could visit with them for their and my own good while they kept a close eye on us.

"The doctor is running a test so it's going to be an hour or two before you see them again," Lydia said. "I'll ask if they can sleep in your room tonight."

I felt my entire body unclench. "Oh my gosh, thank YOU, Lydia!"

"You know you owe me, witch," Lydia said.

"What?!?" I demanded. The last couple of weeks more and more from my dream continued to pop back in my mind—this was one of them. It felt like so much had happened in those critical seventy-two hours.

Lydia's emerald green eyes widened and then looked back and forth like a Kit-Cat Klock as her brow furrowed. "It was a joke, Jolie—you don't owe me anything." Lydia walked back to me. "You need to get a little rest before seeing the twins. This is a good time for a nap." She took the journal and laid it on the table by me and flipped the light switch.

I tossed and turned as well as a woman who just suffered a head injury and given birth to twins could move after all that. Sleep was not happening as my mind kept coming back to the three black kittens, and Lydia's comment that was so familiar—not to mention the ominous edge of their whimsical wolf-and-sheep costumes. The puzzle pieces of the dream I'd had over those seventy-two hours kept coming back to my mind.

I grabbed my journal and the pencil Lydia left for me to trick me into not walking around. I opened the journal, trying to find a blank page.

I started to write the pieces I could remember down. *I've just had the craziest experience—*

My brain put on the brakes. I felt like I had been ready to pour out an entire story on the page, but all I saw now was blackness. I could see in the shaded areas of the first line I wrote, the grooves imprinted from something written on the sheet of paper above it, although there was nothing written on the sheet above. Was a piece of paper missing? If I lightly shaded the paper, I could see the hidden message.

I scribbled darker and continued to use the graphite of the pencil to show me more of the words:

Great-Granny Esme Emerald—Cherokee—gypsy—psychic—casino. My mind lost all the last words as my eyes narrowed on *Esme Emerald*.

That's what I named the twins, I thought to myself, panicking for a moment.

My head started to spin a bit and my mouth slowly opened. How did that get there? I began flipping to prior pages, using pencils to see if other codes lay inside the journal—but I couldn't find any.

"Hey, you're awake!" Lydia walked in with Ava.

Ava came with baby Pria, who was dressed as the cutest little pumpkin seed. Ava sported a dress with pumpkins all over it and *Mama Pumpkin* on the front. She sat next to me with a sorrowful expression as she cradled her baby pumpkin seed.

I was confused at the dichotomy of the fun outfits with the sad faces—also the costumes in November. "What's with the costumes and why do you look so sad?"

Lydia took my hand on the other side. "Jolie, I—"

"What happened to the girls? Are they okay?" I jumped out of the bed and almost knocked Lydia over.

"WHOA!" Lydia yelled, trying to get ahold of my flailing body. "They're FINE—it's NOT the babies!"

As that last statement resonated, I felt the

monstrous rage lessen within me and sank back on the bed. Ava's large eyes had the "chill" look she sometimes had to give me when I went a tad crazy.

"It's Chuck, Jolie. His cancer has progressed and they've just brought him into the ICU."

I felt my body stiffen and my lips tighten into a straight line. *Just like my mom and great-granny and grandma. Wait.* Great-Granny? My mind raced, trying to make sense of things.

"Should I leave you alone?" Lydia glanced from Ava to me.

"I think so," Ava nodded, concerned, shifting Pria.

"I can take her. I'm done with my rounds and off my shift now." Lydia reached for baby Pria. Ava's face remained polite, but her body stiffened visibly.

"I'm a nurse and a mom. I've got this," Lydia assured her.

"Okay," Ava said hesitantly, "but please don't go beyond the desk out there. It's too soon—" Ava started to apologize.

"No need, I get it—I wanted Monty within earshot for weeks too!"

"Thanks," Ava said, kissing little Pria on her head. "You be good for Lydia, lady."

Pria flapped little hands at her mama.

"Are you okay about Chuck? I'm sorry, I didn't think you'd take it so hard." Ava's face contorted with concern.

"No, I mean, I knew he had cancer but then he disappeared again. It's horrible—regardless of how I feel about him, he is my blood. Also, you know me—I somehow feel bad about *not* feeling as bad as I should. But I barely know the man."

"I know—I kind of feel bad that I don't feel worse," Ava agreed. "I don't like disliking someone that much."

"Maybe being moms is softening us?" I asked as we stared at each other for a long moment.

Ava shrugged.

"I'll have to take a bit of time to think on how to deal with Chuck's cancer and the twins while we are also moving our investigation forward."

"Wait," Ava said, "what investigation? You mean who hit your car? I thought Mick already told you all that—"

"No, not that. Look at this." I opened the journal to show Ava what I had found.

"What does that mean?" Ava shook her head, squinting to read the imprinted writing.

"I don't know—it's my handwriting but I don't remember writing it and I don't know why it looks like I wrote it on another piece of paper in pen so it's code in the journal."

"Are you messing with me? It's not Halloween anymore, dummy! Those names!"

"I know." I slumped. "I mean I'm THRILLED the girls were born on Halloween—all three of ours—that's got to be fate, right? But I've never missed the Halloween annual bash before. At least *you* got to wear a cute dress after the fact." I held a hand out, showcasing her cute mama pumpkin dress, then gestured at my hospital gown with a sneer. "And I can't get your three fur babies out my head for some reason. I even thought I saw them running past my door, only looking like the wee little babies they were last year!"

"Whoa, that's super bizarre, you bringing them up." Ava's eyes misted over.

"Why?"

"We thought Delilah had a late fall cold, but we found out she's very allergic to cats." Ava struggled to raise her eyes. "She can take something for visits if we go places like your house, but to have them inside with us twenty-four/seven—" Ava wasn't able to finish.

"We'll take them." I felt as if I were outside my body, committing to something I didn't fully understand.

"But you have eight cats, a husband, and twins—I—I," Ava stammered.

"Nope, I get the feeling those girls somehow saved me and my girls—interesting the number three—three kittens, three babies born on the same day—" I veered off.

"Jolie—EARTH TO JOLIE—" Ava was practically yelling in my ear.

I reactively jerked my hand to my ear to protect it. "Chill!"

"Where are you, girl? Lydia just came in to say I can take you to the cafeteria for some food, and then we can visit Esme and Emerald!"

Ava helped me to a wheelchair and pulled out my black cat slippers to put on my feet.

"Awwww," I said, patting her hand, feeling more at home. Although, I wasn't sure how the three little black kittens would feel about my choice in home footwear. Hopefully, Mick would be okay with my decision to augment our domestic cat population.

As we rode down in the elevator, Ava took a pick out of her bag and began picking out my bird's nest of curls.

"OW!" I yelled. "Get off! It's fine. We're just getting some pudding and the little monsters won't care what my hair looks like—they're bald for goodness—"

"SURPRISE!!!!!" the villagers of Leavensport screamed, all decked out in adorable costumes.

I recoiled, startled, and my extra pregnancy weight made my wheelchair roll backward over Ava's foot.

"OW!" she yelled, grabbing her toe.

"Serves you right for trying to yank out my hair!"

The cafeteria was decorated, tables piled with goodies. A banner that read, "Congratulations, Jolie & Mick!" hung on the wall.

"I was trying to save you embarrassment!

Here." She pulled a witch hat out of her large diaper bag and put it on my head, fixing a few stray curls that hung down and quickly brushing some blush and a wisp of lip gloss onto my lips. "That'll have to do, I guess." She rolled her eyes at my lack of glamour and pushed me out into the room before walking around me to Lydia, who handed Pria back to her.

Lydia grinned at me. "Were you surprised? Got a little more than pudding, right?"

"You two, I swear ..." I replied, playfully shaking my fist at them.

"Hey child," Grandma Opal bellowed in her Macbeth witch costume.

"You look great as always, Grandma!"

She reached down to kiss me on the cheek. "Leavensport couldn't have the All Hallows' Eve bash without you!" She gestured to all the villagers chatting and snacking, many hovering nearby, seeming eager to catch up with me.

I guess being in an accident and almost dying didn't boost my enthusiasm for crowds. My heart started to pound a bit harder and my hands got sweaty. I started to dry my palms on my pink and black cat robe.

"We'll be right back, everyone! Go ahead and enjoy—she'll be here all night—she can't leave even if she wants to!" Ava sang out a BWAAAHAAAHAAA evil laugh as she handed Pria to Delilah then pushed my wheelchair over to a closet, opened the door, and closed us both in it.

"Why'd you push me into a coat closet?" I asked, gesturing at the fall jackets.

"Did you see Nestle and Asher are here in their construction outfits?" Ava asked.

"No, I mean, why would they show up *here*? They don't even pretend to like me."

"I don't know—I keep getting deja-vú," Ava said.

I felt goosebumps rise on my arms. "I can't believe they declared it an accident. It all feels like too much of a coincidence." I felt like my words were dragging a bit as my mind clouded.

"The police came to the scene and looked at everything and questioned everyone," Ava sighed. "According to them, the brakes on the truck failed. All I know is we need to dig more into all of them." She wheeled me to the closet door where I pulled the sliding doors open slightly to see if I could peek at them.

I saw people in costumes in line to get the food that everyone had brought. Lydia had ducked away and quickly changed into the same costume of a wolf in sheep's clothing with Monty as a baby lamb and she was taking some sort of bubbly green punch from a golden goblet at the table.

My mouth fell open. "What's that? What's Lydia drinking from?" I pointed, leaning forward in my wheelchair.

"It's lime sherbet punch. It's freaking delicious,

you should try it," Ava said, glancing around the room.

"No, what's she drinking *out* of?" I pushed the closet door open and rolled myself out into the crowd.

Just then, Keith interrupted my train of thought by hugging me. Then he turned to Ava.

"Hey, Tex." He nudged her, referring to her love of the Dallas Cowboys.

"Pack!" She playfully punched him on the shoulder. I knew it killed her to acknowledge he was a Packers fan, but she played along.

I continued looking at people's costumes as they stood in the line for food and talked. There was a woman in a Cherokee headdress with a leather dress talking to someone in a snake costume, which gave me the creepy-crawlies. I hated snakes. I wondered who they were. Interesting costumes.

"Ahhh-haaaa-haa-haa-haa-haaa!" four witches cackled together, slinking toward me.

"Funny, family," I said, then did a double-take. "Wait, why are there four Macbeth witches this year?"

Grandma Opal rolled her eyes. "Bea decided she wanted to join the gang."

My grandma and Bea had been having off and on issues for the past year—kind of like Lydia and I used to.

"I thought it would be fun to go from triplets to quadruplets!" Bea cackled.

Grandma rolled her eyes again but I smiled and reached for Bea's green hand.

"Thanks for visiting me," I said.

"How'd you know?" Bea asked, surprised.

"I—I don't know how—"

"They say people in comas are sometimes aware of things happening in the room," the woman in the Cherokee costume said, taking off the headdress. With it off, I suddenly recognized that the woman was Marissa, who had become my latest nemesis by opening a deep-dish pizza shop in the village and directly copying the deep dish we served at Cast Iron Creations.

"Jolie, I was so worried about you!" The snake lady leaned over to hug me but didn't take the mask off. I could tell from the bodysuit she was female, though.

"Who are you, anyway?" Marissa asked rudely.

The snake lady grinned and put her finger to her lips and slithered away.

I got a bit of an odd feeling in the pit of my stomach and thought maybe I'd been there too long. Plus, I wanted to see my babies.

"Ava, do you mind taking me to see the girls? We can maybe come back if I feel like it."

"Wow, motherhood clicks in fast—I never thought I'd see the day when something pulled you away from your favorite holiday party."

"You mean the only party of the year I don't complain about." I grinned.

"Well, not too much, but yeah, you were the center of attention this year, so I see why you want to leave." She had pushed me to the elevators. I glanced over and saw Nestle glare at me as the doors closed on us. As we went up, Ava fiddled with her phone, turning on the song *Monster Mash*, and then jamming it back in her pocket. It was the perfect soundtrack for the day.

Ava wheeled me into the maternity ward and I saw my husband sitting in a rocking chair, wearing a doctor costume. I burst out laughing when I saw that the nametag on the costume read "Girl Power!" He was holding Esme and Emerald, who were dressed in the cutest little headdresses with a feather coming out of the back—they were a gorgeous blue color with golden sparkles going through it. I found myself mesmerized by it, then saw their baby feet in moccasins and their tan crocheted sleeveless dresses.

"Where did you get those costumes?" I cried out, reaching for Esme.

"Bea Seevers *made* them," Ava exclaimed. "Can you believe it? She put together those outfits in a couple of days' time while you slept the days away." She pulled out her phone and turned the volume on the Halloween music down some so as not to disturb the little ones.

"Come on, they're sleepy, let's go down and get something to eat." Mick carefully lay the girls, one at a time, in their bassinets. He smiled at each for a moment, then turned and reached for the handles of my wheelchair. "I forgot to tell you! I went home to take a nap and a shower and the cutest little calico cat was outside our garage. She seemed like she was starving and she's just a kitten. I figured what would be one more at this point? I named her Punkin—my Papa Giuseppe never could pronounce the word pumpkin and said punkin instead. I figured that was a nice tribute to him—he was a good guy from what I remember."

My mouth dropped open as Ava caught my eye, grinned, then mouthed T-W-E-L-V-E while holding up both hands then two fingers, reminding me, as if I could forget, that I now had *twelve cats* counting the three black kittens and Punkin.

"No, I want to stay with them a bit longer," I protested, deciding to hold off telling him about the three other kittens we were taking in at the same time we would be bringing two babies into our home—oh well, we had enough love to spread around. "But you go and see the festivities. You've been with them a lot today. I need some mommy time." I lifted my face for a kiss.

"I'm staying," Ava said. "Although, I do think we should go back at some point. They got this cool fortune teller to read our futures!" She squealed in delight.

"Um, that doesn't sound appealing to me," I said, rubbing Emerald's smooth, ruby cheek with my thumb. All of the pieces started coming together from my dream.

"You're no fun," Ava pouted, sitting next to me.

"What's wrong?" she asked after seeing my expression.

"I've told you about the bits and pieces of that weird dream I had while I was unconscious. The ghost kitties, Native Americans in war gear—Imelda was there in a snake costume, Ava. That woman in the cafeteria—who was she?"

Ava shrugged her shoulders. "I don't know, but it wasn't Imelda—she's in prison in Italy."

A loud mixture of hissing and a cackling crow of laugher echoed down the hall. I whipped my head around as the twins both started wailing at once.

"What was that?" Ava asked, shocked.

My brain screeched to a halt and my jaw dropped. "Wait, you heard that?"

Suddenly, I got an idea. I knew how we could trap Nestle in a crime. I knew this would be imperative to help me solve my Great-Granny Esme's murder. That dream was no dream, and Ava and I needed to figure out my ancestry and who that vampire was in the real world once and for all.

The End (or is it?)

Some GHOULISH Recipes (MWUUUHAAHAAAA!)

Witches' Finger Cookies

Taken from https://www.foodnetwork.com/recipes/giada-de-laurentiis/witch-finger-cookies-2229436 **there is a video that shows how to make these on this page!

Ingredients:

- Vegetable oil cooking spray
- 2 cups all-purpose flour
- ½ teaspoon baking powder
- ¼ teaspoon fine salt
- ½ cup (1 stick) unsalted butter, at room temperature
- 1 cup sugar
- 1 large egg, at room temperature
- 1 teaspoon pure vanilla extract
- 28 large sliced almonds
- ½ cup raspberry jam

Directions:

1. Place an oven rack in the center of the oven. Preheat the oven to 325 degrees F. Spray a

rimmed baking sheet with vegetable oil cooking spray or line with a silicone baking mat. Set aside.

2. In a medium bowl, whisk together the flour, baking powder and salt. Set aside.

3. In the bowl of a stand mixer fitted with the paddle attachment, beat the butter and sugar together until light and fluffy, scraping down the sides of the bowl with a spatula as needed, about 2 to 3 minutes. Beat in the egg and vanilla until smooth. Gradually beat in the flour mixture until a dough forms.

4. Using about 1 1/2 tablespoons of dough at a time, roll the dough between your palms into 5-inch-long fingers about 1/2-inch thick. Firmly press a sliced almond into the end of each finger to make fingernails. Make several horizontal cuts, about 1/4 inch deep and 1/2 inch long, in the center of each finger to make knuckles. Press the dough on either side of the cuts to shape the knuckles. Arrange the fingers on the prepared baking sheet and bake until light golden brown, 16 to 18 minutes. Transfer the fingers to a wire rack and cool completely.

5. In a small saucepan (cast iron comes in here using a seasoned cast iron skillet that holds heat is an excellent and yummier way to heat up the jam), heat the jam over low heat until warm, about 2 minutes. Dip the blunt ends of the fingers in the warm jam and arrange on a platter.

Pumpkin Muffins with Streusel

Taken from: https://thenovicechefblog.com/
pumpkin-streusel-muffins/

Ingredients:

Pumpkin Spice Muffins:

- 1 3/4 cups all-purpose flour
- 1 tablespoon pumpkin spice
- 1 teaspoon baking soda
- 1/2 teaspoon salt
- 1 (15 oz) can pumpkin (pure pumpkin puree)
- 1 cup granulated sugar
- 1/2 cup packed brown sugar
- 2 large eggs
- 1/2 cup vegetable oil
- 1 tablespoon vanilla extract

Cinnamon Streusel:

- 1 cup all-purpose flour
- 3/4 cup granulated sugar
- 1 teaspoon cinnamon
- 1/4 teaspoon salt
- 6 tablespoons butter, melted

Cream Cheese Icing:

- 2 ounces cream cheese, room temperature
- 3/4 cup powdered sugar
- 2 tablespoons milk
- 1/2 teaspoon vanilla extract

Directions:

1. Preheat oven to 375°F. Place paper baking cups into the muffin pan. Set aside.

2. Cinnamon Streusel: In a small bowl, whisk together flour, sugar, and cinnamon, add melted butter and stir with a fork until crumbly (can also beat with a hand mixer until crumbly if you need to). Set aside.

3. Pumpkin Spice Muffins: In a medium bowl, whisk flour, pumpkin spice, baking soda, and salt until well combined. Set aside.

4. In a large bowl, whisk together pumpkin, sugar, and brown sugar.

5. Beat in eggs, vegetable oil, and vanilla extract. Slowly whisk in the flour mixture, until there are no lumps. Fill muffin tins 3/4 full.

6. Top each muffin with 2-3 tablespoons of streusel mixture and gently press down.

7. Bake muffins for 18-20 minutes, or until a toothpick inserted in the center comes out clean.

8. Cream Cheese Icing: In a small bowl, beat together cream cheese, powdered sugar, milk,

and vanilla until smooth. If needed, slowly add more milk until you reach a good drizzle consistency.

9. Drizzle the frosting onto the warm muffins and serve immediately!

Halloween Blueberry Mummy Muffins

Ingredients:

Muffins:

- 2 cups fresh blueberries
- Nonstick cooking spray
- 1 ½ cups all-purpose flour
- 1 cup whole-wheat flour
- 1 cup granulated sugar
- 2 ½ teaspoons baking powder
- ½ teaspoon apple pie spice
- 2 teaspoons kosher salt
- 1 ¼ cups buttermilk
- 8 tablespoons (1 stick) unsalted butter, melted
- 1 teaspoon finely grated lemon zest and 2 teaspoons lemon juice, from 1 lemon
- 2 teaspoons vanilla extract
- 1 large egg plus 3 large egg yolks, beaten to blend

Frosting:

- 2 ounces cream cheese, at room temperature

- 4 tablespoons (1/2 stick) unsalted butter, at room temperature
- 2 cups confectioner's sugar

Eyes:

- 24 blueberries (about 1 cup)
- 24 small candy eyes

Directions:

1. Special Directions: Use a pastry bag fitted with a 1/4-inch flat tip

2. For the muffins: Position a rack in the center of the oven and preheat to 425 degrees F. Crush the blueberries in a medium bowl with a potato masher or fork until completely smashed. Lightly coat the cups of a standard 12-cup muffin pan with nonstick spray.

3. Whisk together the all-purpose flour, whole-wheat flour, granulated sugar, baking powder, apple pie spice, and salt in a large bowl.

4. Add the buttermilk, butter, lemon zest, lemon juice, vanilla extract, egg, and yolks to the mashed blueberries and stir until combined and creamy; gently fold into the flour mixture until just combined (it's ok if there are some lumps). Divide the batter evenly among the prepared muffin cups.

5. Bake, rotating the pan halfway through, until a toothpick inserted into the center comes out

clean, 25 to 30 minutes. Transfer the pan to a wire rack and let the muffins cool in the pan for 5 minutes. Remove the muffins and let cool completely on the rack.

6. For the frosting: Meanwhile, beat the cream cheese and butter in a medium bowl using an electric mixer on high speed until light and creamy, about 5 minutes. With the mixer on low speed, gradually add in the confectioners' sugar. Once all the sugar has been added, increase the speed to high and continue to beat until stiff and creamy, about 3 minutes. Transfer to a pastry bag fitted with a 1/4-inch flat tip.

7. Starting from the top of a cooled muffin, leaving a small space for the eyes, pipe frosting from left to right forming crisscrossing ribbons that mimic the wrapping of a mummy. Pipe a small amount of frosting on the back of 2 blueberries and two candy eyes. Place the blueberries, frosting-side down, onto the unfrosted part of the muffin. Top each blueberry with eyes. Repeat with remaining frosting, muffins, blueberries, and eyes.

*Food Network recipes are great because they always give great tips. Here's one from their site I recently found—you all may know this—but I didn't—seems like common sense once I think about it—so that tells you all a lot about me ☺. Anyway—here's the tip ☺

Cook's Note: (FYI—sorry—this is Jodi talking

to you again) I checked to see who the "cook" was and it says "Recipe Courtesy of Food Network Kitchen." What the FREAK? Like, I need to know are we talking Bobby Flay level cook, Rachel Ray? Or is this a cook that just won your latest contest but still doesn't know a lot about cooking or baking? LOL—I've never found out who this cook is—but it does make sense—and YES, I was the person pouring from the bag!

When measuring flour, spoon it into a dry measuring cup and level off the excess. (Scooping directly from the bag compacts the flour, resulting in dry baked goods.)

From the Author

Behind my eyes, a nebula in the shape of a witch's head glowed in the dark part of my mind.

That line from chapter seven is based on a fact—NASA named a nebula Witch Head because it looked like a witch screaming. I personally want to thank so many of you for reaching out to me by email (jrath@columbus.rr.com) or through messenger to tell me how much you enjoy this section of the book that delves more into the process of my writing and the research that goes into the series. You'll find a ton of research in this novella, not to mention the words and phrases in the Chiller font that lead you all to clues relating to how the series will end in the last few books coming up.

Since so many of you have let me know how much you love the process, I figured I'd share with you that this novella had more revisions than any book I've worked on to date. I spent a total of forty-six hours revising this book in three days—that doesn't count the three hours my editor and I met to brainstorm many fixes. I've never tried my hand at writing anything in a supernatural realm, so this proved to be difficult for me, but a ton of fun!

You'll notice a lot of information about the

Cherokee nation in this book. Recently, I've been on a quest to dig more into my ancestry after my ninety-one-year-old grandma told me both her daddy and granddaddy were full-blooded Cherokee that grew up in North Carolina on the reservation. I never knew this before!

Here's a list of the research that went into this book:

Cherokee Nation:

- Clothing worn.
- War attire.
- War weapons.
- Healing rituals.
- Ancestry.
- Symbolism of dreamcatchers.
- Terminology.
- Family traditions.
- Chants.

Supernatural:

- Tarot card reading.
- Time and loss of time.
- Supernatural lore—information on people in comas and those that are unconscious with head injuries.
- Atmosphere.
- Levels of confusion.

- Tricks the mind can play on one when they are unconscious and how that translates to dreams and nightmares.

Halloween:

- Different traditions.
- Costumes.
- Recipes (there are some yummy ones in this book that are also fun!).
- Top Amazon searches for Halloween.
- Different cultural traditions for pumpkin strudel that helped shape the overall story.
- Interesting facts about Halloween from National Geographic's book on weird facts of the season.

Pregnancy:

- Remember, I've never had a child. Luckily, my BFF and editor has had three AND she is a twin herself!
- Third-trimester issues.
- Labor.
- Birth.

And SO much more!

Chicken Cutlet Caper

Two-point-five million dollars' worth of solid gold soap?

Life in Leavensport, Ohio, had been boring for Jolie Tucker growing up. Now, moving into her thirties, life had changed to near-constant pandemonium. Twelve cats, a husband, eight-month-old twin girls, co-owning a restaurant and part-time PI firm, not to mention her helicopter mom, grandma, and aunt—Jolie's life left a lot to be desired. A vacation could not come soon enough!

Jolie and her best friend, Ava Martinez, have been planning a staycation since Halloween, when their babies were born on the same day. They've planned out who in their families will watch their kids while they lie by the Leavensport pool, drinking in plenty of sun and hopefully some fun fruity beverages.

But life has a way of pulling them back into the daily chaos. When Devonte, the manager of Leavensport's local shelter for unhoused people, is found dead, face down in Jolie's famous Cast Iron Chicken Piccata, Ava and Jolie fear that their friend Lia may also be in danger. Lia has been hiding in plain sight from her ex, Jackson Nestle, an unscrupulous local businessman Jolie and Ava suspect is connected to many criminal activities in their village.

Things get extra dicey when one of Nestle's henchmen goes missing along with two-point-five million dollars' worth of gold bars. The criminals of Leavensport are hot under the collar after one hundred grams of gold wrapped in hotel soap packaging that was supposed to have been smuggled through the Villy Crisis Center instead disappears into thin air.

Now, the women have their hands full trying to figure out a murder, find a missing man, and get their hands on the gold before Nestle so they can finally put him behind bars for good!

Will this turn out to be the staycation from Hades?

Welcome to Leavensport, Ohio, where *DEATH* takes a *DELICIOUS* turn!

*******Note to my amazing readers: Right now, Chicken Cutlet Caper is available for preorder and the date is set for October 29, 2022— BUT it will come out late Spring of 2022—I'm just not positive of the exact day yet—so, if you preorder it, then you'll get it A LOT earlier than the current preorder date!*

About the Author

Moving into her second decade working in education, Jodi Rath has decided to begin a life of crime in her The Cast Iron Skillet Mystery Series. Her passion for both mysteries and education led her to combine the two to create her own business, called MYS ED, where she splits her time between working as an adjunct for Ohio teachers and creating mischief in her fictional writing. She currently resides in a small, cozy village in Ohio with her husband and her eight cats.

Other Books by this Author

Book One: Pineapple Upside Down Murder
Short Story 1.5 *"Sweet Retreat"*
Book Two: ***Jalapeño Cheddar Cornbread Murder***
Book 2.5 ***A Holiday Novella Turkey Basted to Death***
Book 3 ***Blueberry Cobbler Blackmail***
Book 4 *Cast Iron Stake Through the Heart*—co-written with Rebecca Grubb
Book 5 ***Deep Dish Pizza Disaster***
Book 5.5 ***A Holiday Novella Yuletide Cast of the Iron Skillet***
Book 6 ***Monkey Bread Business***
Book 7 ***Pork Chopped to Death***

Links So We Can Stay Connected

Be sure to sign up for a monthly newsletter to get MORE of the Leavensport gang with free flash fiction, short stories, two-minute mysteries, cast-iron recipes, tips, and more. Subscribe to our monthly newsletter to keep up to date on the series, for chances to win freebies in raffles, and to be the first to know of sales or promos I'm in. Sign up here: http://eepurl.com/dIfXdb

Follow me on Facebook at https://www.facebook.com/authorjodirath

@jodirath is where you can find me on Twitter

www.jodirath.com is where you can keep up with all the different writing projects I'm working on—currently, I'm in contract for the following writing projects:

Do you have kids, grandkids, or are you a teacher? If so, I'm in contract now to write a Hi-Lo mystery series for struggling student readers called Weeping Willow High. This series is a long-term project but look for the first and second in the series to come out in the next few years. Follow the progress here: https://www.jodirath.com/weeping-willow-high-mystery-series

Do you need a bit more than cozy, clean mysteries in your life? Like to live a bit on the edge from time to time? I've been contracted with a studio to work on a script for a streaming service called *Blurred Mirrors*. This psychological thriller is partially based on a true story from my life. I'll admit to being a bit amazed at all that goes into making a TV show—it's a lengthy, time-consuming project. Also, I LOVE that I have a pen name for this project—here, I'm known as Stormee W. Rath. Follow our progress here: https://www.jodirath.com/stormee-w-rath

Do you like hard-hitting essays with an edge?

Another pen name I write under is J.R. Furi where I collaborate with other powerhouse female writers. Currently, we have one article published with many more to come over time. Follow our progress here: https://www.jodirath.com/j-r-furi

Lastly, you are here for the Cast Iron Skillet Mystery Series—keep up with all the latest on the series here: https://www.jodirath.com/castironskilletmysteryseries

Upcoming Releases

Coming Spring of 2022, ***Chicken Cutlet Caper***
To pre-order on Amazon, just go to
https://geni.us/oiyfJ

*****(Note to my wonderful readers: Chicken Cutlet Caper is currently up for preorder now—the preorder date is October 29, 2022, so as to give me time to finish this next book with other writing projects BUT it will come early—sometime in the Spring of 2022! Thank you all for your continued support of my writing!)

Look for a brand-new cozy series from Jodi Rath coming in 2023!